Solid Ground

Teen EastEnders

Solid Ground
Growing Pains

HUGH MILLER

Teen EastEnders
Solid Ground

DRAGON
GRAFTON BOOKS
A Division of the Collins Publishing Group

LONDON GLASGOW
TORONTO SYDNEY AUCKLAND

Dragon
Grafton Books
A Division of the Collins Publishing Group
8 Grafton Street, London W1X 3LA

Published by Dragon Books 1986

By arrangement with BBC Publications, a division of BBC
Enterprises Limited.
EASTENDERS is a trademark of the British Broadcasting
Corporation

British Library Cataloguing in Publication Data

Miller, Hugh, *1937*–
    Solid ground.—(Teen East Enders; v. 1)
    I. Title II Series
    823'914[F]   PZ7

ISBN 0-583-31088-5

Printed and bound in Great Britain by
Collins, Glasgow

Set in Times

for Morag Bain

1

Den was standing by the fridge with one arm propped on the top. He was gaping at Angie, whose eyes were glinting as hard as her bracelets.

'Me?' Den said. 'Unreasonable? *Me*? It's you that's wantin' to take time off on a busy Saturday night, when I need all the help I can get. Now *that's* unreasonable.'

'You can't see past the end of your own hooter,' Angie snapped. 'I've not had a night off in yonks. You've been away twice this week – '

'Listen,' Den interrupted. 'When I go out I let you know in advance – an' I make arrangements for somebody to stand in whenever I can.'

Sharon had paused on the landing outside, watching them. She had come to the conclusion, long ago, that arguing with each other was like food and drink to those two. They had to do it at regular intervals, just to survive. It was a notion that took some of the pain out of the situation for Sharon.

'It's not as if I want the whole night off,' Angie reasoned. 'Two hours, just long enough to have a drink over at The Lion. That's all I'm askin'.'

Den's eyebrows went up. 'What's wrong with havin' a drink here at The Vic?'

'I told you. Doris Young's havin' her hen night over there. I just want to have a couple of drinks to wish her well.'

'Hen night,' Den growled. He pulled himself to his full height, pointing a finger straight at Angie. 'What you should do is take Doris aside an' warn her what a mistake she's makin'. Bring her over here an' let her see what bein' married's all about. An hour of watchin' us an' she'll get the message.'

Sharon moved away before the real slanging began. She had heard it all before, anyway. Tonight's barney was no different from most of the others. She went downstairs and let herself into the bar. Wicksy, his hair smoothed to perfection, was serving up one end while Lofty, spiky-headed and owlish, dithered at the opposite end.

The place was packed and the buzz of mingling voices was soothing. There might be half a dozen arguments going on for all Sharon knew, but the point was she couldn't hear them.

'You're lookin' very smart tonight, Shar.' It was Pauline Fowler, sitting on a stool beside her husband Arthur. 'That top's new, isn't it?'

Sharon nodded. 'Dad got it for me.' The shade of pink wasn't quite what she would have chosen herself, but she liked the cut and the way the sleeves ballooned at the wrists. 'I picked the jeans myself.'

'Lovely.' Pauline shifted on her stool and nudged Arthur, who was muttering to the man on his left. 'Get a move on with that pint. I want to get back in a minute.' To Sharon she said, 'Michelle's on her todd with the two kids. Mum's turned in early, so she's no help.'

'I'll come over an' see 'Chelle later on,' Sharon said. Michelle was Pauline Fowler's seventeen-year-old daughter, a year older than Sharon and her best friend. Michelle's illegitimate baby had been born a few months ago. Since that time Sharon had seen sad changes in her pal. 'I wish she could get out more, Pauline. She looks so pale an' tired all the time.'

'It's a full time job, havin' a nipper,' Pauline sighed. Her own youngest child was barely a year old. 'I'll see if I can arrange for Michelle to get a night off, once the baby's a bit older.' She nudged Arthur again. 'Come on, you. Playtime's over.'

As they left Sharon turned and glanced in the mirror. She fancied she saw some changes in herself these days, too. She still had the bright, confident features and the mop of blonde hair that made her compulsive viewing for most of the lads · in the district. The difference now, she believed, was in her eyes. Since she had become interested in religion and had been trying to have more compassion for people, she thought her look had softened. On the other hand it could be the new eye makeup.

She turned from the mirror sharply, remembering what the Bible said about vanity. She glanced along the row of faces at the bar. 'Anybody want servin'?'

A man held up an empty glass. 'Pint of Churchill please, love.'

As Sharon took the glass and put it under the pump Angie came through from the back, pulling on her coat. She walked around the end of the bar with tight little steps, the way she always walked when she was annoyed. She smiled tightly at Sharon as she headed for the door.

'See you later, sweetheart.'

Sharon nodded and pulled the pump handle,

watching Angie flounce out through the door. She saw nothing of herself in that woman, yet people often said she was just like her mum. That was just through living with her, Sharon thought. They had mannerisms in common and a few habits of speech, that was all. Time and again she had wondered if she was anything like her real mother.

'There you go.'

Sharon put the frothing pint in front of the customer and took his money. She was ringing it up on the till when Den came through. He was touching his tie and patting his pocket flaps to make sure they weren't turned in.

'Don't worry,' Sharon told him. 'You look neat as a Burton's dummy.' Den's personal smartness was one of his regular obsessions. 'I see you've let Mum have her way, then.'

'Let's just say I was blackmailed, Princess. She threatened to work to rule next week, so *I* wouldn't get any time off.'

'Ooh, we couldn't have that, could we?' Sharon gave him a hard look. 'You've got to have your little bit of relaxation, eh? It don't half make you look tired afterwards, mind you.' Instantly, she wished she hadn't said it.

'Less lip, eh?'

Sharon sniffed haughtily as Den tightened his tie and wandered off along the bar. She was always dropping jibes and wisecracks about his girlfriend. She knew she shouldn't because it was uncharitable and mean-spirited. On the other hand, she sometimes felt she was striking a blow for Angie, rather than for herself.

A small cheer erupted by the corner door as Edith Hunter came in, tidy and smiling in her Salvation Army uniform. She had an armful of copies of the War Cry. People began buying them without being asked, dropping their money into her tin as she moved across the room.

'Give us The Old Rugged Cross, Edith!' somebody shouted.

'Nah! Make it Abide With Me!' a woman called.

Another man yelled that he wanted to hear The Holy City. There was a sudden babble of opposing requests, some of them flippant, most of them genuine. Edith nodded steadily, handing out her papers. When she had sold the last copy she put her tin on the bar and held up a hand for order.

'Right then,' she said, 'you all know the drill. A show of hands decides what one I'll sing for you, and it's a pound in the tin. All right?'

As the voting proceeded Lofty sidled up beside Sharon, who was standing at the corner of the bar. They watched as Edith called out the names of hymns and counted the hands that shot up in response.

'She's a great girl, eh, Shar?' Lofty said. 'Heart of gold. Forever helpin' people an' cheerin' them up.'

'That's what Christianity's all about,' Sharon murmured. She wanted to be like Edith, to be a ray of sunshine in people's lives. She wasn't sure she had the right temperament, though. Everything about Edith was outgoing, she never seemed to be thinking about herself. In her own view, Sharon never seemed to be thinking about much else.

'Here we go.' Edith snatched up her tin again and

11

passed it round. A pound was swiftly collected in fives, tens and twenties. The room went quiet as Edith stepped to a space that had been cleared in the centre of the throng. She cleared her throat softly, then folded her hands in front of her.

The hymn they had chosen was Abide With Me. As Edith began to sing Sharon felt a little pang at her heart. The purity of the voice and the sentiment of the words were a perfect unity. Sharon experienced something like a yearning, a powerful need for something, perhaps peace. She adored the notion of peace, spiritual and physical. Peace was something she had never really known, except at odd, fleeting moments.

There was loud cheering and clapping when Edith finished singing. Sharon was close to tears. She quickly dabbed at her eyes as Edith came across and leaned her elbows on the bar. She smiled at Sharon.

'That was lovely, Edith.'

'Thank you.' Edith pointed to one of the back shelves. 'Do you think I could wet my whistle with a lemonade? I've a few more pubs to visit yet, so I'll have to keep my tubes in order.'

Sharon promptly picked up a bottle and uncapped it, wondering how old Edith was. Whatever peace or serenity she had found in her religion, it had made her ageless. She could be twenty-five or thirty-five; maybe younger, maybe older.

'On the house.' Sharon poured the lemonade into a glass and handed it to Edith.

'God bless.' Edith sipped and let out a sigh.

'That's better.' She cocked her head at Sharon. 'So what kind of week have you had?'

'So-so. I read that booklet you gave me. Twice, in fact.'

'And what did you think?'

Sharon frowned. 'I get the message all right, but . . . Well, I don't know how to put it into action, if you know what I mean.' The booklet was called *A Guide to Practical Christianity*. Ever since Sharon had been talking to Edith about religion, she had been loaned a number of leaflets and handed a lot of advice.

'I think it's mostly down to keeping your eyes open for an opportunity,' Edith said. 'If you're out to serve your own ends, it's always easier to spot a chance. To want more for yourself than other people always comes more naturally.' She grinned. 'It's not impossible to reverse the process, though.'

'I think it'd be pretty hard for me,' Sharon confessed. 'I'm dead selfish. I know I am.'

'Do you want to change?'

'Yeah,' Sharon said. 'Definitely. But it's a habit, bein' selfish. As bad a habit as smokin' I suppose – an' just as hard to give up.'

Edith nodded. 'But you've taken the first step. You've admitted your selfishness, and you really want to do something about it.' She sipped her lemonade and put down the glass again. 'The next step is to exercise your charity. Get some muscles on it.'

'How?'

'Take a hard look at people. Say to yourself, "What can I do to improve that person's life?"

13

There's nobody doing so well they don't need a bit of help.'

Sharon thought about it. She could imagine trying, but she could also imagine not wanting to be bothered, what with all her own problems.

'We had a great example of practical Christianity the other week,' Edith said. 'This man over on Cuthbert Road, he'd been trying to locate his brother for fifteen years. Then he heard that the Sally Army operates a service to help people find missing relatives. It doesn't always work out nice and smoothly, but this case did. We located his brother for him inside four days. It was magical, just to see their faces.'

Sharon's mind had veered sharply off the subject. *Missing relatives*, she was thinking. For years she had wondered if, one day, she would find her real mother and father. During the last year or so she had just about decided it was impossible. But now Edith was telling her there was a service . . .

'Erm, this service, Edith. Do they do it for anybody?'

'Of course. Anybody at all.'

'Only, I heard about somebody, an adopted person. She wants to find her real folks. Would the Army do that?'

Edith shook her head. 'No, that's not our territory, Sharon.'

'Oh.' She tried not to let her disappointment show. Just for a moment the old hope had been back, the yearning she used to have, like the feeling she got listening to the hymn. 'I was just wonderin', that's all.'

'There's no need for us to operate a service like that, anyway,' Edith said. She finished her lemonade and stood back, picking up her tin. 'Nowadays adopted people can find out who their real parents are without any trouble.'

Sharon's heart thumped. 'Really?'

'Oh, yes. They just write off somewhere. I'm not sure where, and for a few pounds they can have a copy of their birth certificate.' Edith smoothed her coat and straightened her bonnet. 'Must dash, I've a carload of papers to sell yet. See you next week.'

'Yeah, right,' Sharon said absently. She returned Edith's little wave, her eyes distant as she ran the stunning news through her mind again. This was amazing! She could actually get hold of her birth certificate. She could have it in black and white, the names of her parents and an address that would put her on their track. *Fantastic*!

'Oi. Princess.'

Sharon turned and saw Den staring at her.

'Trances aren't allowed while you're supposed to be workin'.'

'I was thinkin' about somethin' . . .'

'Well do your thinkin' when you're on your own time. There's three blokes standin' up there with their tongues hangin' out from lack of beer.'

Sharon moved along the bar and began serving. She was on automatic pilot now, going through the mechanical motions of pulling beer and taking money, while her brain seethed with its new knowledge. The dream that had been beyond her reach was in front of her now, on a plate, ready for the taking.

'Did anyone ever tell you you're a bit like the young Marilyn Monroe?'

Sharon stared at the smirking, spotted youth leaning on the bar, waiting for her to fill his glass. He looked like one of the BEFORE pictures on a Valderma advertisement.

'No,' she said coldly. 'Who's Marilyn Monroe?'

Buried fantasies were stirring in her. She used to imagine her parents had been a beautiful, carefree young couple, terribly successful, madly in love with each other and their baby. One day they had a car crash and were both killed. But the baby was thrown clear and survived. Then she had the bad luck to be adopted by Den and Angie Watts and brought up in a mouldy Victorian pub in Walford.

'Ta,' she said, passing across the drink and ignoring the wad of fivers the lad was flashing. 'Anythin' else?'

'Just a smile, darlin'.'

She snatched the note he offered. 'I'm out of stock.'

At the till she paused, recalling how often she had wondered if she'd actually seen her parents and not known it was them. It was possible. She might even have brothers and sisters. At times the thought tormented her, at others she had been excited by it. But *now* . . .

'You're flamin' dreamin' again,' Den hissed, coming to the till. 'Get your act together, Sharon. If you want to work here for readies I expect to see a bit more action.'

Sharon took out the change and slammed the till shut. She'd get her act together, all right. He'd see action. First thing Monday she would find out how to go about getting her birth certificate. That was Phase One. When that was done she'd get on the trail and do all she could to reduce the misery of being the adopted daughter of two people who didn't deserve to have a family in the first place. Just seeing her parents, or even only her mother, would put her on solid ground. She'd feel like somebody, instead of just a substitute person, a token.

'Thanks, gorgeous,' the spotty one said as she gave him his change.

'That's all right, handsome,' she grunted, realizing that what she was planning was very selfish. Even so, she had to go along with the impulse, it was too strong to resist. She was glad she didn't have to explain it to Edith.

2

Because the schools had broken up for the summer holidays Sharon had plenty of free time. But the holidays also meant there were a lot of her friends on the streets, and that morning they were getting in the way of her plans.

She had gone no further than the corner of Bridge Street when a girl from her class flagged her down and began showing her the albums she'd bought from the market record stall. Sharon dropped a few swift oohs and aahs then excused herself, explaining she had to get something for her dad. Two minutes later she bumped into Jenny Chilton. Jenny was heavily in love with a boy at Walford College, and she never missed a chance to talk about her grand passion.

'I've been out with Jim five times since I saw you last,' she said breathlessly. '*Five* times in six days – imagine.'

Sharon could imagine, all right. The boy was a gawky beanpole with all the charm of an old grey sock. 'You're really gettin' serious, aren't you?'

Jenny nodded, fluttering her eyelashes. She used so much mascara, Sharon observed, that her lashes looked like two big spiders twitching. 'I'll tell you somethin' in confidence, Shar. He's been talkin' about marriage.'

Sharon stared at her. 'That's daft. You've the rest

of your teens an' twenties to enjoy yet. What's the sense in gettin' married an' spoilin' everythin'?'

The winsome smile left Jenny's face. 'I don't look at it that way,' she said.

'You'd be givin' up your freedom.'

'Freedom?' Jenny squeaked. 'Is that what you call it?'

'Yeah. Bein' single is bein' free.'

Jenny gave a little snort. 'Bein' free to be lonely, you mean? Free to go out an' work to support yourself, free to scrape along on your wages an' free to wind up on the shelf when your looks go – '

'Well, your business is none of mine anyway,' Sharon cut in, anxious to end the conversation and get moving. 'I just hope you don't let yourself get carried away without thinkin' things out first.' She moved away, even though it was obvious Jenny wanted to talk some more. 'I've got to rush. Maybe I'll see you round at the community centre later on.'

She left Jenny standing there and hurried on, feeling rather two-faced about cautioning somebody else on the danger of getting carried away with something. Without even considering any arguments against what she was doing, she had allowed herself to get well carried away with this plan. Nothing would stop her, either.

'Not long now, kid,' she murmured, feeling a delicious little thrill. It was great to be moving, to be doing something positive. Sunday had been endless. She had roamed about the pub and around the square, restless and downright grumpy if anybody spoke to her. She kept imagining what it would feel like just to *know* who her folks were, let alone actually see them. And now, at long last, she was about to take the first step towards cracking the mystery.

It took her less than ten minutes to get to the High Street; she would have been even quicker if two more school friends hadn't tried to delay her. Outside the glass-fronted office block by the traffic lights she stood for a minute and read the names on the row of aluminium plates by the door. The Citizens' Advice Bureau was on the second floor.

Sharon was nervous at first. She had never been in one of these places before, and she wasn't sure how she should put her request. She hadn't given it a thought until she was standing by the counter, waiting for somebody to attend to her.

A friendly-looking woman in jeans and a tee-shirt came forward and smiled at her. 'Hello. Can I help you?'

Sharon's mind suddenly blanked. She should have rehearsed this! 'I – umm . . .' She coughed a couple of times, thinking furiously as the woman continued to smile. 'It's, ah, it's about adoption . . .'

'You look a bit young to be wanting to adopt a baby,' the woman said.

'No, it's not me. I mean it's not *for* me . . .' Sharon felt her cheeks warming. 'It's a friend. She's a bit shy about askin', so I said I'd do it for her.'

'I see.' The woman leaned on the counter and folded her hands. 'So what's the problem?'

Sharon coughed again, pretending to dislodge a stubborn frog from her throat. 'Well, this friend, she's adopted, see. She's never known who her real parents are. Then somebody told her there was a way of findin' out nowadays. I was wonderin' if you could tell me how to go about it.'

The woman nodded. 'I'm sure I can. Excuse me for a minute.' She went away to a back room.

This is it! Sharon thought. Any second now she would have the key. She rubbed her palms on the seat of her jeans to dry them. She realized she was trembling.

The woman came back with a leaflet. 'We've only got our copy of this, I'm afraid. But I can give you the information you need, if you care to write it down.' She pushed forward a pad and ballpoint. Sharon picked up the pen in shaky fingers as the woman peered closer at the leaflet, running one polished nail down the page. 'Ah. Here's the bit I was looking for. We can get that down for starters. For your friend to obtain a copy of her birth certificate, she would write to this address.'

Sharon began writing, hoping she'd be able to read her nervous scrawl when she got outside. She hesitated over the spelling of Titchfield, then put it down the way it sounded, figuring she could look it up later. All she wanted was to get that address on paper before the woman changed her mind and said she couldn't have it.

When she had finished writing she tore the page off the pad and stuffed it in her pocket. 'Thanks a lot.' She pushed back the pen and pad and made for the door.

'Hang on,' the woman said. 'That's not all.'

Sharon frowned at her. What more could there be?

'Your friend would have to go through a counselling process before she could get her birth certificate. It's nothing too serious, mind you. She'd simply speak to certain people who would explain the size of the step she's taking, and they'd want to satisfy themselves she wasn't making a big mistake.'

Sharon fingered the paper in her pocket. This wasn't at all what she had expected. All she wanted was to get an address and write to the people. Counselling had a bad ring to it. What would they want to know? What kind of snooping would go on?

'I think the best thing you can do, come to think of it,' the woman said, 'is go to the adoption people at the council's Social Services Department and ask for a copy of this leaflet. Do you want to write down the name of it?'

Sharon's head was spinning, and she was trying to fight off a sinking feeling in her stomach. 'Well, yeah, I suppose so . . .'

As she reached for the pen the woman said, 'I presume your friend is over eighteen?'

Sharon's hand froze. 'Pardon?'

'An adopted person has to be over eighteen before he or she can get a copy of their birth certificate.'

The words sank in like little hammer blows. 'Oh, I see,' Sharon said. Her mouth was turning dry. 'Yeah, she's well over eighteen. She's nineteen, actually.' She pulled forward the pad and wrote down the title of the leaflet as the woman read it out to her.

Back on the street she stood and looked about her, with no urge to walk one way or the other. She had never felt so crushed in her life. She was forcing back tears, biting her lips as the cruel truth set in. There was no way to find out who her parents were after all. No hope, not for at least two years, which was an eternity. Even then she would have to go through counselling, and maybe they'd say she couldn't have a copy of the certificate, anyway.

She had no idea how long it took her to get back to Albert Square. Outside the Queen Vic she leaned on the wall and stared at the market stalls, not really seeing them. On the slow walk back she had tried to dig out some consolation from her despair. There were other things in life, she reminded herself. She was a busy person. She'd need to rehearse regularly with the band they were getting together. Then there were the preparations for Michelle's wedding to Lofty – Sharon was going to be a bridesmaid, so there was a lot to do in that direction. She could think of dozens of things that needed her time and attention. It would be easy to distract herself until the pain wore away.

But none of that washed with Sharon. Now, more keenly than ever, she ached to find her parents. There had to be a way. Nothing was impossible – Lofty was always telling her that, even though he hardly ever found it possible to do anything without fouling up.

Sharon pushed herself away from the wall. So what *was* the way to find out, now it was obvious she couldn't do it the official way? She stared at Pete Beale, handing out a stream of cheery patter as he sold housewives fruit and vegetables off his stall. It was all right for him – it was all right for everybody she knew, come to that. They all knew where they came from, they had their solid ground.

She kicked a squashed apple into the gutter and shuffled along to the side door of the pub. As she let herself in she realized something. Out of all her misery and frustration, only one thing alone was clear. She was hooked on this mission of hers, more hooked than she'd been on anything, ever.

At half-past eight Den took a break from the bar to watch television in the sitting room. He was slumped on the couch, watching a gun-toting detective chase a villain across a roof as Sharon came in and sat down beside him. Without taking his eyes off the set Den slipped an arm around her shoulders. Sharon pretended to watch the film for a minute. When it got to a no-action scene she turned to Den.

'Dad . . .'

'Mm?' He was still watching the box.

'You know I've asked you a couple of times about who my real mum and dad are?'

Den looked at her. 'Yeah. An' I told you we're your real mum an' dad.' He craned his neck forward and pecked her cheek. 'An' we are. We love you as much as anybody could. You're our family an' we're yours.'

Sharon sighed softly. 'I can see that, but . . .'

Den turned down the sound on the set. 'But what?'

'Well, it would do somethin' important for me, I don't know what, but it *would*, if I could just know me mum's name, even.'

24

Den's eyes hardened a shade. 'What's this all about, Princess?'

'Just what I said. It would help to – oh, it's hard to put into words. I just feel odd inside, not knowin' . . .'

Den sat forward, keeping his eyes fixed on her. 'Now just listen to me.' He had switched on his Let's-Drop-This-Nonsense look. 'You're legally the daughter of Den an' Angie Watts. No other person has a legal claim. The woman that had you – she never even knew you. There was no bond. Do you understand that? We *are* your real mum an' dad, the two people who truly wanted you an' truly love you. Right?'

'But all I'm askin' is – '

'That's the end of it, Sharon. Not another word on the subject.' Den's hard look softened as he leaned close to her again. 'Don't go complicatin' somethin' that's simple. You're with two people who've raised you an' would do anythin' in the world to make you happy.'

Anything except tell me the name of my mother, Sharon thought. She sighed again and stood up. Den watched her go out, then turned his face to the television again.

Angie was working behind the bar, serving up drinks and rapid-fire banter to the locals. She was handing a drink to her best friend, Kathy Beale, as Sharon came into the bar and stepped up beside her.

'It suits the shape of me face,' Angie said to Kathy. 'I tried it out upstairs earlier, but I didn't have the bottle to let the punters see it. Maybe I will later on, when I get a bit more used to it.'

'What's that?' Sharon asked.

'Hello sweetheart. I'm tellin' Kath about my new way of puttin' on make-up.' She wrinkled her nose. 'An old lady needs all the help she can get.'

If she cared at all, Sharon would agree with that. Angie was getting on a bit. She'd soon be forty.

'I use a beige foundation,' Angie said, talking to Kathy again, 'an' then I put on a layer of this pinkish powder I've got. Then it's the old pink blusher on the cheeks, with just a dab on the forehead an' chin . . .'

Sharon moved away. There was no point in trying to pump Angie. She hadn't really been sure she would try. The answer would be the same as Den's – you're ours and that's all that matters. Besides, Sharon had just had another idea.

'I'm slippin' over to see Michelle for a bit,' she called to Angie. 'Won't be long.'

She crossed the road to number forty-five and tapped the back door before she let herself in. Michelle was alone in the living room, flopped back in a chair and leafing through a magazine. She looked up and smiled as Sharon came in.

'Hi. I was hopin' you'd pop over.'

Sharon sat down at the table. 'How's Vicki?'

'Sleepin', thank the Lord. I don't know where babies get their energy from. She was fightin' sleep for half an hour before she finally gave in.'

Again, Sharon noticed how pale her friend was, and how much older she had begun to look. She was still a young girl, but motherhood and its pressures had stolen a lot of her youthfulness.

''Chelle, I was wonderin' if you'd do me a favour.' Sharon thought it was as well to come straight to the point.

'Oh, I see.' Michelle said it with a mock scowl. 'So you didn't come over because you were pinin' for my company.'

'Course I did, but I thought I'd kill two birds with one stone, like.'

'Fire away.'

'It's about my parents, the real ones I mean,' Sharon said. 'I've been tryin' to find out who they are.'

'How'd you go about that?'

'I thought there was a way, but I ran into a dead end.' She explained about her chat with Edith from the Salvation Army, then what happened when she visited the Citizens' Advice Bureau. 'The thing is, now I've got the bit between me teeth . . .'

'Yeah,' Michelle sighed. 'Sounds just like you. Once you're on to somethin' you stick to it. What do you want me to do?'

'Try an' find out for me – who they are, I mean. Just my mum's name would do, an' where she came from.'

Michelle blinked. 'How am I supposed to do that?'

Sharon leaned forward, lowering her voice. 'Try an' get somethin' out of your mum or your gran. Or better still your Aunt Kath – she should know somethin', she's best mates with Mum.'

'Oh, I don't know, Shar . . .' Michelle shook her

head slowly. 'They'd want to know what I was askin' for. They'd smell a rat. You know what they're like.'

'But would you try anyway, eh?'

'What do you want to know for?'

'I just do. It's hard to explain.'

Michelle frowned at the carpet for a minute. 'All right,' she said finally. 'I'll give it a whirl. But don't expect too much.'

'I won't. Bless you 'Chelle, you're a mate.'

Michelle was frowning again. 'Listen – what makes you think Den an' Angie know who your real mother is? Have they ever said they do?'

'No,' Sharon said. 'But I'm positive they know.'

'How come?'

'Because they've never said they *don't* know.'

Michelle grinned. 'Proper little detective, aren't you?'

'I'll learn to be,' Sharon said. 'All I need is one good clue.'

'Yeah, well. Like I said, I'll try, but that's all I can do.'

Sharon smiled warmly. 'I'll keep my fingers crossed for you,' she promised.

3

'Lofty!' Den yelled along the bar. 'Try not to be a banana all your life! Stack the boxes of mixers up *this* end, next to the shelves.'

Lofty straightened, rubbing his back. 'I think I've ricked somethin',' he mumbled.

'You can nip over an' get Dr Legg to rub somethin' on it when you've finished here,' Den said. 'Meantime get them shelves stacked. We're openin' in ten minutes an' there's half an hour's work to be done yet.'

'Right, Den. I'll see to it.'

Den disappeared through to the back. Lofty turned and stared at a shaft of sunlight slanting through the window. He shouldn't have volunteered to do an extra morning in the pub, he decided. He would much rather be outside in the sun. He could have gone for a walk up the park with Michelle and the baby.

The thought of Michelle made his stomach all fluttery. It was still hard to imagine she was going to marry him. A bright girl like that, so assured, so positive in everything she did, belonged with a man who could match her. Lofty, by his own reckoning, was her complete opposite. But facts were facts. He'd started out feeling sorry for her, because of the baby. His concern had turned into love. And when he asked her to marry him she said yes –

eventually. So that was that. Whatever Michelle saw in him, Lofty hoped it would be enough to hold her for good.

He began moving the crates of ginger ale, tonic water and fruit juice to the other end of the bar. As he worked his mind drifted to Michelle's baby, Vicki. He'd have no trouble being a loving father to that little angel. He didn't care who the real father was. There were people who believed it was him. That was their problem, they could believe what they liked. All Lofty cared about was making sure Vicki had a good upbringing, and that her mother could take pride in the kind of dad her baby had.

The thought of being a father to somebody stopped him in his tracks. It often did, lately. He was standing there, staring at the sunlight again, when Sharon came downstairs and into the bar.

'You seen an angel or somethin'?'

Lofty jumped. 'Cor, Shar, you gave me a start.'

'Somebody needed to,' she snapped. 'You looked like your engine had stopped.'

'I was dreamin'.' He turned and began stacking bottles on the shelves. 'In a bit of a mood about somethin' are you, Shar?'

'What makes you think that?'

'It's just a hunch.'

For a moment Lofty tensed, sure she was going to give him an earful. But she didn't. Instead she stamped off round the bar and let herself out by the end door.

'Definitely somethin' up,' Lofty murmured to a half-empty crate. Sharon had been acting stiff and prickly since Tuesday. It was Friday now and she

30

was still the same, as if somebody was drawing sandpaper across her nerves. Lofty had asked Michelle if Sharon was upset about something, but she'd only shrugged.

'Women,' he sighed.

After painful years of trying to understand feminine moods and motives – and nearly always getting it wrong – Lofty had decided females were ruled by some zig-zagging cosmic energy that men couldn't tune-in to. Right or wrong, it was a theory that helped him put up with one more baffling feature of a puzzling life.

While Lofty continued to stack the shelves, Sharon was making her way across to the little fenced-in garden at the centre of Albert Square. She could see Michelle was there already, sitting on a bench in the sunshine, gently rocking the pram beside her.

'How did you get on?' Sharon asked before she had even sat down.

'I didn't,' Michelle said.

'What?'

'I got nothin'. Nobody knows a thing.'

Sharon stared accusingly. 'You mean to tell me that after three days diggin' you've come up with absolutely zilch?'

'That's what I'm sayin', yeah.'

'God almighty!'

Michelle glanced into the pram to make sure Vicki was still asleep, then she turned to Sharon. 'Look, don't make it sound as if I've let you down, Shar. I did all I could. I asked Mum, Gran, Aunt Kath an' even Uncle Pete. They don't know a thing. Den an'

Angie have never talked about where you came from. Not to my family, at any rate.'

'It's incredible.' Sharon gazed down down at her fingers, twisting them together irritably. After a moment of chewing her lip she looked up at Michelle again. 'You're absolutely sure, are you?'

'Yeah, I'm positive,' Michelle said patiently. 'I've got myself a lot of funny looks for goin' on about your real parents, Shar. I've had Mum goin' on at me about pryin' into other people's business. Gran did a bit of barkin' about it, too. I've put myself out for you, an' I'm convinced they don't know a thing. You'll just have to accept that.'

Sharon was silent for a minute. Finally she put out her hand and squeezed Michelle's arm. 'I'm sorry. It's just the disappointment. I was hangin' all my hopes on what you'd find out. Thanks for tryin' anyway. An' I'm sorry you had a bit of bother.'

'That's what mates are for,' Michelle said. 'To put themselves to a bit of effort for you, when you need it. But Shar . . .' She paused. 'I've got to say it – you're makin' too much of this. I know you've got your reasons for wantin' to find your parents, but it's gettin' too much of a grip on you. The last couple of days you've been goin' about with nothin' else on your mind. That ain't healthy.'

Sharon had no answer. She was obsessed, she knew that, but there was nothing in her to resist the way she was. The night before she had lain in her bed and listened to Den and Angie having another one of their rows. Suddenly the need to find her parents had blazed in her. It was a flame of longing so strong it had made her cry. Afterwards she had prayed fervently that when the morning came, Michelle would have something for her, a pointer she could follow. Now she was back where she started, empty of hope.

She stood up. 'I'm helpin' in the pub this mornin',' she said. 'Maybe we can get together this afternoon. Get a bit of sun about us.'

'I've got the clinic at three,' Michelle said. 'But if I'm back in time, maybe I'll see you. Vicki'll want feedin', though, an' she'll have to be changed an' all the rest of it . . .'

Sharon shrugged. 'Well, if I don't see you today I'll come over tomorrow.' At the gate she paused. 'Thanks again, 'Chelle.'

Going back to the pub, she thought how much of a difference it would make if Michelle was her mate again – properly, not just part-time. Michelle's duty as a mother had practically taken her out of Sharon's life. The old days were gone. Along with them had gone the security of having at least one close friend to confide in and occasionally lean on. The loss made the present bleakness worse, but Sharon knew no way out of it. She was depressed beyond tears.

The second she walked into the bar Angie pounced.

'Over here, young lady. I want a word with you.'

Sharon groaned. 'What now?' Angie was in her heavy-mother stance, head held stiffly back, hands on hips. 'I'm not in the mood for arguin', Mum.'

There were no customers in the bar yet, so Angie didn't bother to keep her voice down. 'I met Kath when I was out at the shops this mornin'. She reckons you've been askin' people if they know anythin' about where you were adopted from.'

'Well I haven't.'

'You asked your dad on Monday night. I know that for a fact.'

'He's the only one I asked.' That was true enough, as far as it went, so Sharon didn't feel she was lying. 'Who did Kathy say I asked?'·

'She didn't go into details. She just said she thought that's what you'd been doin'.'

Sharon went behind the bar, feeling Angie's eyes fixed on her. 'What's the big deal, anyway? It's not as if I don't have a right to know certain things.'

'We've been into all this before,' Angie said. Behind the tight features there was a shimmer of anxiety. 'Why's it so important to know?'

If Sharon had wanted to answer she might have told Angie how much of an outsider she felt, trapped against her will with two people who regularly fought, cheated and lied their way through a marriage that was nothing but a mockery. Even their child was a substitute for the real thing. But Sharon didn't feel like saying any of that. She wanted to be left alone.

'Darlin' . . .' Angie's voice had softened. She came and stood close, irritating Sharon with her perfume. 'You're not thinkin' you'd like to leave us, or nothin' like that?' The anxiety was on the surface now, wrinkling the corners of Angie's eyes. 'You know you mean everythin' – '

'Yeah, sure I do.' Sharon glared coldly at Angie for a moment then strode to the other end of the bar as a customer came in. 'Mornin',' she said with brittle cheeriness. 'What can I get you?'

Angie remained where she was, looking openly sad.

The idea came just after ten o'clock that night. When it came, Sharon remembered something she read in one of Edith's religious pamphlets. The writer said that despair, if it was kept quiet, could soon give a person a very clear mind. To make it work, all you needed was a glimmer of hope.

For most of that day and all evening Sharon had known, even though she was despairing, that there was a trace of hope still alive in her. It was stubborn hope, senseless hope, but it was there. And bingo! she had suddenly come up with an idea.

Her gloom was lifting rapidly as she tiptoed from her room to the top of the stairs and listened. They sounded very busy in the bar. That meant nobody would be upstairs until well after closing time.

Sharon crossed the landing to Angie's room and went in. By the dim glow of the bedside lamp she stood and looked around, wondering where to start. She had maybe an hour and a half, and she might need all of it, for Angie's belongings were an Aladdin's cave. She never threw anything away, or so it seemed. As she gazed about her, something at the back of Sharon's mind told her this was a really wild shot, but she ignored the warning. If there was a clue about her parentage to be found in the Queen Vic, it would be in this room.

Downstairs, Den was trying to ignore Angie, who was in one of her mother-hen moods.

'Just stop a minute an' listen to me!' she hissed. 'We've got to talk about this!'

'Terrific,' Den snarled, barely moving his lips. 'I've got a pub full of punters wantin' to give me their money, an' you want me to stop servin' them an' have a heart-to-heart.' He slapped down the handle on the lager pump and started filling a glass. 'Why don't you just go along that end an' ease the traffic jam a bit, eh?'

'I will when you listen to me!'

Den handed over the pint and took the customer's money. 'Right,' he said, turning on Angie. 'Ten seconds, that's all I can spare you. What's up?'

'I already told you – '

'So why are you tellin' me again?'

'Because you don't seem to get the message. We've got to have a long talk with Sharon. There's somethin' wrong. She's tryin' to find out who her real parents are. Tryin' hard, if I'm any judge. Now wouldn't you say it's high time we got to the bottom of whatever's eatin' her?'

Den shook his head. 'I don't think anythin' of the sort, Ange. She's a teenager. Teenagers go through phases. You did. I did. They wear off, don't they? Just leave well enough alone. Don't go encouragin' her little dramas.'

Angie bunched her fists at her sides. 'You're an insensitive swine!'

'I know,' Den murmured. 'Anybody can tell that from the company I keep.'

'An' what's that supposed to mean?'

Den put a finger to his lips. 'Ssh, dearest. Your foghorn's takin' the froth off everybody's beer.'

Angie looked ready to hit him. 'No wonder that poor kid upstairs is feelin' dodgy. Who wouldn't, with a father like you?'

'Ah, but you make up for all that, don't you, Duchess? All that gentle charm of yours, an' your quiet, patient style.' Den nodded to a customer who was waving his glass. 'Excuse me now, will you? Chat time's over. I've work to do – an' so have you.'

Red-faced and furious, Angie struggled to keep a bright expression as she began serving again. She would have to do something about Sharon, even if Den wouldn't help. She didn't like the way their daughter had turned so vague and secretive lately. She was bad-tempered, too, and it was all tied up with this business of trying to find her parents. Angie was sure of that, and it scared her.

'Cheers, love.' She smiled stiffly and slid two drinks across the bar. As she took the money she glanced at the clock. If she got a spare few minutes, she decided, she would go upstairs and have a little talk before Sharon went to bed. It might do them both a lot of good.

By ten-thirty Sharon was beginning to despair again. For a start there was just too much stuff to get through before her time was up. The wardrobe, cupboard and drawers were crammed with boxes, bags and cases full of 'sixties and 'seventies junk.

'It's hopeless,' Sharon groaned, staring at the collection around her feet. She had already been through the corner cupboard and put all the things back. Now she had carefully laid out the contents of two drawers on the floor. There were striped and spangled dresses no bigger than sweat shirts, huge silver rings and pendant necklaces, a half-used box of cosmetics and a whole carton of well-scratched singles with titles like "Have I the Right?", "I Get Around", "Twelve Steps to Love", and lots more, by artists with names like Julie Rogers, The Four Pennies, the Nashville Teens and a dozen others Sharon had never heard of.

None of it helped. She had hoped to find documents of some kind, perhaps a letter. *You're mad!* she told herself angrily, piling the stuff back into the drawers. *Completely mad!*

When she had closed the drawers she stood back, shaking her head. All she had learned was that Angie bought just as much rubbish in the old days as she did now. She glanced at the wardrobe, wondering if it was worthwhile taking a look.

'Might as well,' she sighed.

Feeling very foolish now, she opened the doors and scanned the shelf under the row of skirts and dresses. There were two vanity cases, some handbags and an old shoe box. She decided to start with a vanity case. A swift rummage revealed more half-used cosmetics, ancient nail-varnish bottles, perfume sprays, a manicure set and a box of lace-edged handkerchiefs. Sharon slammed the case shut and snatched out the second one.

'More garbage,' she grunted, opening the lid.

This one had a collection of old birthday cards, brown-edged snapshots of Angie as a young girl, two talcum flasks and an assortment of odd earrings. Sharon was on the point of dumping it all back in the case when she saw something in a tiny elastic-topped pouch at the back. She pulled it out and felt her heart thump against her ribs. It was a pocket diary. She had heard Angie tell Kathy that she'd once tried keeping a diary, but kept forgetting to put things in it. Sharon's heart thumped even harder when she saw the gilt-printed year on the cover – 1969, the year she was born.

She thrust the stuff back in the vanity case, threw it on the shelf and shut the wardrobe. By the bedside lamp she began flicking through the diary with trembling fingers.

There were very few entries. The first one referred to an appointment with a hairdresser. The next two recorded birthdays. Then, panting softly, Sharon stared at the fourth entry:

> Today we were told we can have
> the baby with us within a week.
> Very excited. Still scared Iris
> might change her mind.

Iris! Her mother's name was Iris! Sharon gulped back her excitement. Iris who? She almost dropped the book as her fingers sped through the pages. There were no other entries, apart from two more birthdays.

Sharon felt like screaming. She went through the diary again, but she could find nothing else. Then she realized there was a tiny clip holding down the last few pages. It was an address section. Sharon fumbled open the clip and began turning the pages. Unlike the rest of the book, this part was crammed with entries. There were names she knew, many more she didn't. Then, feeling a great joy swell like a balloon in her chest, she found it. The entry was on the very last page, right at the bottom with a red circle around it:

Iris Pope
17a Gimble Crescent
Bethnal Green

Sharon froze suddenly. The downstairs door had opened. Noise from the bar surged up the stairs. Sharon looked around quickly, making sure everything was the way it looked when she came in.

'Oh, no!'

There was a scarf sticking out of a drawer. She darted across, tucked it in, then let herself out on to the landing, just as Angie began climbing the stairs.

'Are you there, sweetheart?'

Keeping her back to the wall, Sharon slid along to her own room door, feeling glad she had left it open. She whirled inside and pushed it gently shut.

'Sharon? Are you in your room?'

Angie's footsteps came along the landing. A moment later there was a soft tap on the door. Sharon struggled to control her breathing. 'Yeah?' She hoped her voice sounded sleepy enough.

'Are you in bed, love?'

'I was just fallin' asleep.'

'Oh.' There was a pause, then Angie said, 'Sorry I disturbed you, darlin'. Sweet dreams, I'll see you in the mornin'.'

Sharon sat down on the bed, clutching the diary

to herself. She couldn't believe this had happened. She'd cracked it! There was no thought of where she went from here; for the moment it was enough that she had found what she had searched for.

'Iris Pope,' she whispered softly. She raised the diary to her lips and kissed it.

4

Angie had breakfast ready by half-past eight. Den came into the kitchen scratching his head and looking stunned. He dropped into a chair at the table and yawned.

'Mornin', bright eyes.' Angie turned from the worktop with his plate. 'Nice to see you looking so fresh.' She put the food in front of him. 'Get that down you while it's hot.'

Den clicked his tongue a couple of times and made a face. 'It feels like somebody crept in durin' the night an' carpeted my throat.'

'Serves you right for drinkin' all night with that bunch off the market.'

'Don't exaggerate.' Den looked at his egg, bacon and sausage as if something unspeakable had been set before him. 'I wasn't up all night. Only half the night. An' I wouldn't have stopped up at all if it hadn't been for big Paddy Russell. He *insisted* I joined them in a late one.'

'You should have walked past him an' held open the door.'

'Walk past him?' Paddy Russell was a sixteen-stone Belfast man who was easily offended. 'Walkin' past him's like passin' a bull in a corridor.'

Angie went to the door and called out to Sharon. 'Hurry up, darlin'. Breakfast's goin' on the table.' She turned to Den, dropping her voice almost to a whisper. 'I want us to have a talk with her before you go downstairs, so hang around until she's finished eatin'.'

'Oh, for cryin' out loud . . .'

'I don't care what you say. It's a matter for both of us to attend to, not just me.'

'You know what I think about all this – '

'Yeah,' Angie snapped. 'An' you're wrong.' She always knew when she could have the upper hand. Hangover mornings were especially good. 'We're gettin' this sorted out before openin' time, an' that's that.'

There was no sound from Sharon's room. Angie went out to the landing and knocked on her door. 'Sharon? Come on, lovey. Show a leg.' She put her ear to the door and listened. 'Sharon?' There was still no response. Angie opened the door and looked in. The room was empty.

She rushed back to the kitchen. 'She's gone out!'

Den was still staring glumly at his food. 'So?' He glanced at Angie. 'She's gone out early before. It's the holidays, an' she does her own thing durin' the holidays. She's most likely gone to early rehearsals with the flamin' band, or somethin'.'

'She's never gone out this early before.'

'There's always a first time.' Den pushed his plate away. 'I can't tackle that. My stomach's not on duty yet.'

'Never mind your bleedin' stomach!' Angie hissed. 'Where's Sharon gone? What's she up to?'

'My crystal ball's not workin', either.' Den stood and scratched his head again. 'You're goin' over the top about nothin'. Eat your breakfast.'

Angie stared at him. She looked stricken. 'You just don't care, do you? Our daughter's been actin' weird for days, now she's disappeared an' you just shrug it off!'

'Hang on,' Den warned her sharply. 'I *do* care about Sharon, I care a lot more than you an' some other people give me credit for. But carin' an' over-reactin' aren't the same thing. What if she *is* curious about where she came from? She's bound to be, now an' again. Anybody that's adopted would be. But you're makin' out it's some big crusade she's on.'

'I'm sayin' – '

'An' where's the calamity in her goin' out early? It's nothin', yet you're goin' up the wall about it. What're you tryin' to do? Put a bit of soap opera into your life?'

Angie, pale without her make up, pursed her lips until they were as white as her cheeks. She turned away and stared out of the window.

'That's it,' Den sighed. 'Go into one of your huffs.' He looked at his watch, scratched his head one more time and walked out on to the landing. On his way downstairs he called, 'It's not Sharon you should be worryin' about, Ange. It's yourself.'

Sharon got to Bethnal Green before nine o'clock. The night before, lying awake and trying to think what to do next, she decided it was perfectly possible that her mother still lived at the address in the diary. Lots of people stayed in the same house for most of their lives – like Lou Beale, the Fowlers, Ethel Skinner and plenty of the others in Albert Square.

She had brought along Den's A to Z and stood outside the tube station studying it. As far as she could judge she was about half a mile from Gimble Crescent, as the crow flies. Which probably meant, with all the winding and criss-crossing streets between there and the station, that it was nearer a mile on foot.

She looked about for a taxi, but there were none in sight. With the street guide folded open she began walking. She hoped Iris didn't go out to work, otherwise she would miss her and perhaps have to wait around all day. Even if that happened, Sharon wouldn't mind. She could spend the time wandering around the streets where she might have grown up, if things had worked out differently.

She got lost after ten minutes. Somehow she had taken a first right-turn instead of a second, or something like that, she wasn't sure. She stood on a street corner and tried to work out where she was now. That took another five minutes, because for a while she couldn't figure out which way she was facing.

She arrived at the west end of Gimble Terrace at twenty minutes to ten. As she rounded the corner the last traces of early cloud drifted away from the sun. Sharon took that as a sign.

So this is it, she thought, standing and gazing along the two curving rows of Edwardian houses. They were poor-looking properties, most of them with several doorbells and name cards by the front doors. There were children playing on the dusty pavements and a few old women leaned out of upstairs windows, carrying on conversations at the tops of their voices.

Sharon stuck the A to Z in her pocket, crossed the fingers of her right hand and started walking again, reading the house numbers as she went. *Please*, she prayed silently, *let her still be here*.

Number 17 was halfway along the crescent. Sharon climbed the front steps and examined the names by the bells. There were a lot of foreign looking ones, but no Pope was listed. There was no mention, either, of a number 17a.

She went down the steps again and peered through the railing at the basement flat. The number was hand-painted, faded and flaking, but it was clear enough – 17a.

Suddenly, Sharon couldn't move. Here she was, right outside the cherished address – but what was she going to do? She had skirted any fantasy about this moment. Since starting out on her search she hadn't even tried to imagine what her mother looked like; she wanted it all to be fresh and new. She hadn't rehearsed any approach. It was worse than that time in the Citizens' Advice Bureau. Much worse. She was paralysed by shyness and a fear of rejection. What would she *say* if she went down the steps, knocked that door and Iris Pope opened it?

After standing by the railing for a couple of minutes, wavering from one half-formed idea to another, she suddenly did what instinct had told her the first time she stood on a diving board. She shut her mind and propelled herself forward.

She took the steps two at a time and knocked the door three times, sharply, before she knew what her hand was doing. She stood back, drawing her fingers swiftly through her hair and forcing herself not to think. She was in at the deep end, she would tackle things as they came.

Seconds passed but nobody came to the door. She knocked again and waited. There was still no answer. After a third try and a wait of nearly a minute, Sharon accepted that there was nobody home.

As she walked the streets beyond Gimble Crescent, looking for a café, she decided it might be a good idea to rehearse some sort of approach, after all. If she didn't, there was every chance she would just stand there, dumbstruck, with her mouth hanging open – which wasn't the best first impression to give her mother.

'Hello, are you Iris Pope?' she murmured, checking how it sounded. 'You don't know me, do you? Well, I'm your daughter.'

That wasn't bad, but it might be too blunt, too startling.

'Hello. My name's Sharon,' she tried again. 'You don't know me, but we've a lot in common. I wonder if I could come in?'

She decided that made her sound like some kind of teenage con-artist.

'Iris Pope? My name's Sharon. I've been wanting to meet you for a long – '

'There's places for kids what talk to themselves,' an old man grunted, shuffling past her. Sharon blushed, dug her hands in her pockets and decided to rehearse in silence.

The time passed slowly. She found a hamburger

47

bar and had brunch there, which took up less than half an hour. An hour was passed going round two department stores and a record shop. After that she just wandered, getting back to Gimble Terrace at five past twelve. She reasoned that her mother might only have been out shopping, or, if she did have a job, she might have come home for lunch. The possibility that her mother didn't live there at all was kept firmly out of Sharon's mind.

There was still no answer to her knocking. The fourth time she rapped the door an elderly woman put her head over the railings.

'She's out, love. Won't be back till about six. She works up the component factory.'

'Oh. Thanks.'

The woman was still standing there as Sharon came up the steps. She looked a lot like Lou Beale, Michelle's gran.

'Was it somethin' urgent, love?'

'No,' Sharon said. 'It can wait.' She crossed her fingers again as she said, 'Does Iris Pope live down there?'

The woman's eyes widened. 'Iris? Oh, no, dearie.'

Sharon fought down her disappointment. 'Do you know Iris?'

The woman was looking embarrassed. 'Are you a relation, or somethin'?'

Sharon hesitated then said, 'No. But I've a message for her.' Best not to say too much, she thought.

'Well, Iris Pope moved out of here about two years ago . . .'

'Do you know where she went?'

The woman nodded, still looking uneasy. 'Hickson Street. Number eight, as I remember.'

Sharon couldn't hide her excitement. 'Is that near here?'

'Yes, but – '

'Could you show me how to get there, please?'

'I could, love, but there'd be no point.' The woman cleared her throat. 'Iris passed away just before Christmas.'

The words darted about Sharon's head as she tried to defy their meaning. Passed away. Passed away. *Passed away*. The truth couldn't be resisted. 'You mean she's dead?'

'I'm afraid so, dear.'

There was no feeling in Sharon, just the abrupt dullness of shock. Her vision swam and her legs began to buckle.

'Here, are you all right?' The woman grasped Sharon's arms. 'Have a lean on the fence, you've gone terrible pale.'

Sharon heard the blood sing in her ears. The dizziness cleared as quickly as it had come. Emotions swept through her. The awful sense of loss came first, then the slicing pain of grief. She clasped her hands to her mouth, stifling a sob as tears welled and ran along her cheeks.

5

The woman's living room was small and tidy. The sideboard was covered with framed pictures of children; on the wall above them was a large black-and-white photograph of a man and woman in old-fashioned wedding clothes. There were two huge overstuffed armchairs that took up most of the floor space between the table and the fireplace. An embroidered motto over the mantelpiece said, EAST, WEST, HOME'S BEST. It was a grandmother's room, complete with bundled knitting on the table and the smell of lavender polish.

'Just you sit there, love. I'll put the kettle on.'

Sharon sat on the edge of an armchair, dabbing her eyes with a tissue. She felt sick now and weak, the way she did after a bout of 'flu.

'What's your name?' the woman called to her from the tiny kitchen.

'Sharon.'

'I'm June.' She came back into the living room and stood by the table. 'Feelin' better now?'

'A bit,' Sharon said. 'Sorry I cracked up like that . . .'

'You was upset, it's only natural to take on that way.' June tidied her knitting then said, 'Iris must have meant *somethin'* to you, then?'

Sharon didn't want to explain, she knew she would start crying again if she did. 'It was just the shock. My friend that sent me with the message – she talked about Iris quite a lot. It was just like I knew her.'

That seemed to satisfy June. She came and sat opposite Sharon, absently brushing the wrinkles from her floral apron. 'I was friendly with Iris for years. Not close mates with her, nothin' like that, but we had many a natter on the street. She moved out of the flat because the damp got so bad. That was in 1984. I never saw her much after that.' She sighed. 'It's sad when you hear about people you know passin' on. But we all have to go some time, don't we?'

'It's not so bad if they've had a long life,' Sharon said. Tears were threatening again. She took a deep breath to steady herself. 'How old was she?'

'Well . . .' June shrugged. 'Hard to say, lookin' at her. Round about my age, I suppose. Seventy or so.'

Sharon stared. 'Seventy?' That would have made her mother fifty-four when she was born! 'She couldn't have been that age, surely . . .'

'Older maybe.' June stood up as the kettle began to whistle. 'I'll not be a minute.'

Sharon closed her eyes tightly for a moment, trying to grasp what she had been told. It just wasn't possible. How could her mother have been over seventy when she died? Women that age didn't have teenage children. There was no way –

Then light dawned. Sharon leapt off the chair and went through to the kitchen. 'June – did Iris have a daughter?'

June nodded. 'She's called Iris, too.' She finished

pouring the boiling water into the teapot and put on the lid. 'That'll be ready for us by the time I've got the cups, saucers and biscuits out.'

'Where does Iris live?'

'Islington, I think.' June smiled as she took down two cups and saucers from a shelf. 'At my age, you don't need much to keep you goin'. A couple of biscuits an' a cuppa in the middle of the day's all I need. I can remember a time when – '

'Islington? Are you sure?' Sharon saw June frown and realized she had almost barked the question. 'I'm sorry, I didn't mean to be rude an' cut you off like that. It's just that I think it's the other Iris Pope I was meant to see.'

'Oh . . .' June thought for a moment, drumming her fingers on the draining board. Then she shook her head. 'It wouldn't be her, love. She hasn't lived hereabouts for about fifteen years. An' her name hasn't been Pope for a long time.'

'Can you tell me anythin' about her?'

'She's a bad lot, I can tell you that much.' June set the cups carefully on the saucers. 'Never anythin' but trouble to her poor old mum.'

Sharon ignored that. Old people were always disapproving of younger ones. 'Do you know if she had any children?' Her mind was beginning to race, narrowing the facts to a certainty.

'There was a baby, yes,' June said. 'Born before she was married. She had it adopted, though.'

Hallelujah! Sharon thought, keeping her face straight.

'It was a right carry-on. Less than a year after she had the kiddie adopted, she went an' married its

52

father, Reg Porter. Everybody knew it was his. He was the only bloke she ever went with.' June sniffed. 'Another bad 'un, that Reg. They moved to Hackney when they got wed, but the last time I saw young Iris she told me they were in a flat in Islington.'

It felt marvellous to be back on the trail. Sharon stood there nodding, alert to every word June said. 'When did you see her last?'

June took some biscuits from a tin and put them on a plate. 'It was about a month before her mother died, I suppose. Last November, I think. I met her on the corner of Hickson Street. Said she was worried about her mum's health, but if you ask me she was worried about where the old lady's insurance money would go.'

'I'm pretty sure she's the one I'm supposed to see,' Sharon said. 'Do you know whereabouts in Islington she lives?'

June shook her head. 'No idea, love.' She began pouring the tea. 'It must be pretty important, this message you've got for her.'

Sharon nodded, impatient to drink the tea and get moving again. 'It's important, all right,' she said. 'Very important.'

It was after 2.30 and the crowd in The Vic was thinning. Den was in the cellar changing a barrel. Angie was trying to get away from the attentions of Teddy Hardacre, a middle-aged romeo with a face like warm putty who chatted her up every time he caught her on her own.

'You could do worse than nip out for an evenin' with me, Angie. Straight up, I know how to give a girl a good time.' Teddy was leaning across the counter, trying to keep his remarks confidential, but at the other end of the bar the big Jamaican, Tony Carpenter, was grinning and shaking his head. 'I've been around a bit in my time,' Teddy continued. 'I've got a lot goin' for me.'

'I'll say you have,' Angie said. 'Your hair's goin', your eyesight's goin' – '

Teddy couldn't be insulted. 'We could go to this Indian restaurant over in Poplar where they know me. They do a Vindaloo that'd knock your head off. What do you say, eh?'

Angie leaned close. 'I'll tell you what I say. I don't want anythin' to do with a bloke whose idea of showin' a girl a good time is to take her out an' get her head blown off.' She marched away to clear glasses at the other end of the bar, leaving Terry to fidget under an onslaught of chuckling from Tony Carpenter.

Angie was stacking glasses on a tray when Sharon came in. She made straight for the back but Angie stopped her.

'Stay right there, Miss. I want to talk to you.'

'I'm busy, Mum. I'll talk to you later.'

'We'll talk now, or as soon as I've got this lot cleared away. Sit down over there.'

Sharon tutted loudly and dropped on to a stool by the corner table. She sat staring sullenly at the wall as Angie finished with the glasses.

'Right,' Angie said, turning from the sink. 'If any of you lot want servin', give us a shout.' She came round the bar and sat down across from Sharon. 'Now, I'm not about to start a row with you, but I want you to explain yourself to me. An' I want the truth.'

'About what?'

'Everythin'. The way you've been behavin' lately, an' what you went out so early for this mornin'.'

'I've had a lot on my mind,' Sharon said impatiently. 'What with the band rehearsals, Michelle's weddin' comin' up, all that.'

Angie placed her forearms firmly along the edge of the table. 'I said I wanted the truth.'

'That *is* the truth.'

'You haven't been to a rehearsal for over a week. I asked Wicksy and Kelvin. An' Michelle's weddin's not until the end of September, so there's been nothin' urgent for you to do in that direction.' Angie lowered her head and stared at Sharon. 'Now – the truth.'

Sharon set her jaw stubbornly. 'What's it to you what I do?'

Angie looked as if she'd been slapped. 'What? I'm your *mother*. I'm entitled to know.'

'You don't behave like a real mother, do you?'

'Now don't start all that again – '

'You're raisin' your voice,' Sharon interrupted. 'People are listenin'.'

'I don't give a monkey's who'd listenin'!' Angie checked herself suddenly, realizing she was losing her temper. 'Listen, just tell me what's wrong, will you?'

'Nothin' at all. You're imaginin' it.'

Sharon stood up abruptly and walked away. Angie swivelled on her seat, watching her. As Sharon went behind the bar Den appeared from the back.

'Hello, Princess,' he said brightly. 'How's things?'

'Fine. Everythin's just great.'

Sharon went through to the stairs and Den looked across at Angie. 'See?' he said. 'I told you.'

Later, when she had changed into a dark skirt and white blouse, removed her make-up and tied back her hair to complete her "responsible" image, Sharon took a notebook and pencil from her school-bag and left the pub.

The police station was busy when she got there. Three bikers were being quizzed by a surly-looking plain-clothes man. An old woman was tearfully explaining about her missing parakeet. A drunk by the desk was being held upright by two constables while he told the desk sergeant he'd taken too much cough medicine that morning.

'It affects me this way,' he said, swerving away from the desk as one policeman let go for a moment. When he was propped on the desk again he said, 'See, it's something they put in it. I know I shouldn't have tried to drive the car, but I mean – I mean, well, I can't get done for havin' cough syrup in my veins, can I?' He belched softly. 'I'm not a drinking man, officer. Ask anybody.'

'We asked the landlord at the Unicorn,' one of the constables said. 'He said he wouldn't serve you any more, you'd had too much even when you went in there.'

The man considered the information with a wobbling head. Finally he pulled himself to his full height, swayed dangerously for a second, then said, 'I want to speak to a lawyer.'

A young constable came from behind the desk

and approached Sharon. 'What can we do for you, love?'

'I was wonderin' if I could speak to a policewoman, please.'

'What's it about?'

'It's – well, it's a project I'm doin', an' I was told the police would be the best people to talk to. I think I'd be more at ease with a lady.'

'Hang on.' The constable went back behind the desk and picked up the telephone. He murmured something into it, nodded a couple of times and put it down. He beckoned to Sharon. 'Down that passage, love, third door on the right. Inspector Lampshire can spare you a few minutes. Just knock an' wait.'

Sharon thanked him and went along the passage. She stood for a moment outside the third door, collecting herself, trying to look like a serious-minded young woman. Then she knocked.

A woman's voice told her to come in.

Sharon was surprised. She had expected an oldish woman, probably a bit like a headmistress, with a craggy face and her hair in a bun. Inspector Lampshire was nothing like that. She was young, with stylishly cut honey-blonde hair and very attractive features. Her white police shirt looked as if it had been specially tailored for her.

'Good afternoon,' she said, standing and holding out her hand. 'I'm Sarah Lampshire.'

Sharon shook her hand. 'Sharon Watts,' she murmured.

'Sit down then, Sharon, and tell me all about it.'

Sharon had been rehearsing ever since the idea

occurred to her. She settled herself in the chair opposite the desk and put the notebook and pencil squarely on her lap. 'I'm doin' a holiday-time project for school,' she said. 'We all got different ones – mine's about tracin' missin' persons.'

The inspector nodded.

'Well.' Sharon cleared her throat and looked at the inspector squarely. 'The way I'm plannin' to do it, I'm goin' to take an imaginary case, say a person missin' in one of the London districts, an' then describe the process of findin' them, just to show how it's done.'

'Very interesting. So you want me to give you a few pointers, do you?'

'It'd be a big help. I don't even know how to begin.'

Inspector Lampshire sat back and folded her arms. 'Get your notebook ready, then, and I'll tell you all I can.'

Great, Sharon thought, flipping open the notebook. It had worked. It was amazing what a bit of desperation could do for the imagination and the nerve. She poised her pencil over the page and looked up expectantly at Sarah Lampshire.

6

'She wants for nothin',' Angie told Kathy Beale. 'She's the best-dressed girl round here, she gets more pocket money than most an' we give her plenty of freedom. A lot of kids would give an arm to be in her position.'

They were standing outside The Vic by Pete Beale's fruit and vegetable stall. Kathy was helping to lay out the display while Pete brought boxes from the lock-up by the pub.

'It's not my business to make comments,' Kathy said. 'But I know how you feel, love.'

'You're my mate, Kath. I'm tellin' you all this hopin' you will say somethin' – somethin' that'll help.'

Kathy put the final orange on top of a pyramid she had built and turned to Angie. 'It's not *things* Sharon needs. It's not freedom, neither. She needs a bit of stability around her. It's not somethin' I haven't told you before, when you've asked.'

'For her sake I try to make things look better than they are . . .'

'She's not a mug, Angie. The best thing that could happen is for Sharon to walk into the kitchen an' catch you an' Den havin' a kiss an' a cuddle – for real.' She paused, seeing that the truth was hurting Angie. But she had asked for it. 'I'll tell you somethin' else. Not long ago, Sharon told our Ian she was scared Den would leave home for good.'

The distress was putting furrows on Angie's brow. 'She might not be far wrong. Him an' that bird of his have set up a really neat little world of their own. One of these days he might just decide to stay there full time.'

'There you are, then,' Kathy sighed. 'There's no sense tryin' to sort out Sharon, when it's your marriage that needs fixin'. You're drivin' the kid away. What makes it worse, from your point of view, is she might have an alternative somewhere. She's certainly lookin' for it, if you ask me.'

'Yeah.' Angie shifted her heavy shopping bag from one hand to the other. 'She was off out early this mornin' again. That's two days runnin'. God, Kath, what am I goin' to do? I can't get Den to take this seriously. He reckons there's nothin' to worry about.'

Kathy leaned against the stall. 'What you've got to do is start by lookin' at the picture squarely. Sharon's got friends, nice clothes, money in her pocket. It don't amount to sod all, because she can't walk in the house without findin' you two bawlin' abuse at each other, or Den havin' a sneaky phone call to his bit of stuff, or you gettin' tanked-up on gin. What's needed is a bit of stability in the home, Angie. You'll only cure what's hurtin' Sharon when you clean up the mess *you're* in.'

'That's a bit like tellin' a leopard to switch to stripes,' Angie said. 'We've tried makin' a fresh start, Den an' me. But somehow, we always end up as bad as ever. We're fixed in our ways.'

'An' you'll pay for it.' Kathy patted Angie's shoulder. 'It'd be great if I could tell you somethin' really comfortin', love. But facts have got to be faced.'

As they talked, Sharon was sitting in the reference section of an Islington public library. There were sheaves of paper all around her. She had heard of electoral rolls before, but she had never realized how much slogging was needed to get through them. She had been searching for over an hour, but so far she had come up with only two entries under the name of Porter, and neither one had the right initials.

She sat back, glancing again at the notes she had made in Sarah Lampshire's office. To trace a missing person, the police and other authorities made searches of the electoral rolls, court registers, the records of the social services, and the local registers of deaths and marriages.

Sharon had decided the quickest and most reliable source of information would be the electoral roll. Now she wasn't so sure. There were a lot of voters in Islington, and she couldn't even narrow the search by restricting it to one district, let alone one street. Her mother and father could be living in any part of the borough. The search might take her all day and part of the next day, too.

Inspector Lampshire had told her something else. 'Footwork usually gets more results than any other method.'

But there had to be a clue first, some idea of where the footwork would do most good. Sharon knew there was no shortcut, even though she had begun to long for one. She would have to slog on through the close-printed pages in front of her until something turned up.

It was almost thirty minutes later that it did turn up, and Sharon nearly missed it. Her eyes had grown tired and began skidding down the columns of names. Something jarred in her, a warning that she had skipped something vital. She blinked, starting at the top again. Her finger stabbed against each name, keeping her alert. Halfway down the page she found what she was looking for. PORTER I. was entered above PORTER R. opposite the address: FLAT 4, 29 LAMPTON CLOSE. Sharon snatched up her pencil and jotted down the address.

She handed back the wad of papers to the girl at the desk, thanked her and hurried outside. The bright sun made her blink as she took the A to Z from her shoulder bag and flipped through the index. When she located the street name she turned back to the map section and began tracing Lampton Road.

Nothing worthwhile is ever gained without effort. The proverb, learned from one of Edith's leaflets, came back to Sharon with grim clarity. Lampton Close was miles away, dead at the centre of a maze of smaller streets and lanes.

'Just my flamin' luck,' she groaned, fishing out her sunglasses.

That morning she had left the pub in such a hurry she'd forgotten to bring her purse. The discovery was made when she was already on the Underground, whizzing towards Islington. She had exactly thirty-eight pence in loose change at the bottom of her bag, so taxis were out. So were buses. She didn't even have the tube fare to get back to Walford.

'Here's where the footwork begins, kiddo.'

An hour's walking left her hot, leg-weary and very thirsty. Outside a dingy cafe she peered through the smeared window, trying to find out how much it would cost her for a cold drink. The cheapest, according to the hand-written menu card, was forty pence. That took care of that. She would not only learn a lot about heatstroke and blisters, she would find out what it was like to be dehydrated.

It was almost midday when she found her way through the bewildering tangle of streets that surrounded Lampton Close. She found herself in a grimy cul-de-sac, a U-shaped cluster of buildings two and three storeys high. There were occasional demolition gaps, giving the place the appearance of a gigantic, decaying row of teeth.

Her parents must be pretty hard up, Sharon thought. This was a place for losers. Discarded beer cans, rubbish bags and torn cartons lay in sullen clusters on the pavements and in the gutters. The hot air carried whiffs of decaying refuse. The grafitti, which was everywhere, lacked anger, it was more about defeat and loss.

Sharon took out her pocket mirror and peered at herself. Her face looked boiled and the fringes of her hair were plastered to her forehead and cheeks. She would have liked five minutes in a ladies to freshen up. Instead she made do with a brisk comb and a touch-up to her lipstick. When she had dabbed her face and wiped her hands with a tissue, she took

63

a deep breath and started walking, looking for numbers, feeling the excitement mount.

Number 29 was no dirtier than the others. A skinny little boy with sticky-looking hair sat on the top step, eating a Mars bar. Sharon smiled at him. He glared back, chewing steadily.

There were no bells by the door, no name plates. Sharon smiled at the boy again.

'Could you tell me where Mr and Mrs Porter live?'

The boy shut his eyes tightly and opened them again, as if he was telling her something in code.

'Do you know the Porters?'

The door swung open suddenly. 'What's the trouble?' A woman with mean little sparrow eyes and soap-starved skin was standing there, one hand on the door, the other on the hip of her grubby overall.

'Oh, no trouble,' Sharon said, noticing the woman had a terrible squint.

'What're you pesterin' Damon about?'

Damon? Sharon cleared her throat. 'I'm looking for Mr and Mrs Porter. I understand they live here.'

The woman made a funny face, unaware that she looked hilarious without it. 'Oh, you *understand* they live here, do you?' she mocked. 'If you're talkin' about Beef Brain an' his missus – no, they ain't here any longer.'

Sharon took instant, sharp offence. Who did this crone-faced bag think she was, talking about her father that way? How could her opinion of anybody be worth a toss? As she felt herself begin to fume the woman spoke again.

'I suppose you're a council snooper, are you? It's

64

not bad enough people get no help from you lot, you have to come round givin' them more troubles than they've got already.'

Sharon took stock swiftly. She had wanted to make a good visible impression, so she'd put on her dark blue two-piece suit and a pale blue blouse with a no-nonsense collar. She *could* be taken for an official of some kind. Even the modest make-up helped; it made her look older. *Here goes*, she thought, stepping nearer the woman.

'As a matter of fact,' she spat, 'I *am* from the council. I'm an environmental inspector.'

The word "inspector" always put a chill through people. Sharon saw the woman's eyes lose some of their glare.

'Is this child yours?'

'What if he is?' The voice had lost its rasping edge, too.

'Just thank your lucky stars your name isn't on my list for today. I'd expect you to show me his current dental inspection record.'

'His what?'

'And his monthly head-lice check report. Together with his blood-test card.'

Now the woman looked scared. 'I wasn't told he had to have all them things . . .'

'It's the law, Mrs – what's your name?'

'Pavitt. What's all this about the law?'

'You can be prosecuted for neglect, under the new regulations.'

'Oh my Gawd!' Mrs Pavitt's hand slapped against her heart. 'We wasn't told nothin'! I swear it, if anybody'd let on, we'd've – '

'Ignorance of the law is no excuse,' Sharon said sternly, glad she had remembered that one from her Civic Affairs classes. 'Now.' She fished out her notebook and pencil. 'I want some information from you. About the Porters.'

Mrs Pavitt glanced warily at the notebook. 'But what's all this about Damon? I mean, is there goin' to be any trouble, or what?'

'We'll get to that. Have the Porters moved?'

'Yeah. They used to live on the first landin' when they was here.'

'How long ago did they move?'

Mrs Pavitt's face seemed to clench for a moment as she raked her memory. 'About March, some time. I can remember because the Electricity Board men were round, cuttin' off them that hadn't paid-up on the red bills. The Porters skipped the same week.'

'Have you any idea where they went?'

'Well, I saw Iris Porter down the DHSS not long since, so they can't be far away.'

Sharon took a long, frowning stare at Damon, then looked at Mrs Pavitt again. 'Are you sure you can't be more helpful than that?'

Mrs Pavitt got the message. Sharon's look was saying, *Play ball with me, maybe I'll play ball with you.*

'I think I heard my old man say Reg Porter's been usin' the George, over on Bright Lane.'

Sharon wrote it down. 'Anything else you can tell me?'

'No. Nothin' at all. So help me.'

'Right. Thank you very much, Mrs Pavitt.' Sharon turned to leave.

'What about, you know, what you was sayin' about Damon here . . .'

Sharon paused, making her expression as severe as she could. 'We'll have to get around to you sooner or later. We get around to everybody, in time. I'd advise you to get him to the school dentist, fast as you can, and see the welfare people about getting the rest of him checked over. Then you'll have nothing to worry about, will you?'

She turned and walked carefully down the steps, still seeing Mrs Pavitt's fearful, grateful expression.

At the corner she stopped and consulted the A to Z. She located Bright Lane and was about to head off in that direction when it occurred to her she didn't even have the price of a drink.

She leaned on a wall and considered the situation. She had come close, but unless she got incredibly lucky she could go no further today. She had come with the worst disadvantage of all, no money. As Den always said, 'Money's where it's at. It can't buy you happiness, but neither can poverty. With plenty of dough you can be miserable in comfort.'

So, impatient as she was, Sharon decided the best thing to do was start on the long, long walk back home, get an early night, then come back in the morning with plenty of cash and, perhaps, a new and more deliberate disguise.

She had to smile. The council-official routine had worked a treat. Who was to say another false front or two wouldn't come in useful? She was pretty sure she would track down her family tomorrow – but there was no harm in being prepared for more obstacles. Besides, she thought, it was great fun being somebody else. She never realized she had it in her.

7

The dream came towards dawn, when troubled sleep gave way to a deeper rest that seemed to make her body float. She was in front of a house with drab, chipped plaster and cracked windows. A man was at her side, gently urging her forward. She climbed the steps and when she was near the top the door slowly swung open.

The woman who stood there wore a threadbare dress and a cardigan with frayed cuffs. She was thin and pale. And she was beautiful. She moistened her lips nervously and said, 'Hello, Sharon.'

'Hello.'

The man touched Sharon's shoulder and she stepped close to her mother. She saw years of terrible sadness in the blue eyes. When she tried to speak there was a great swelling in her throat. She tried again and suddenly she was holding Iris, squeezing her and crying happy tears on her shoulder.

The scene faded into another. They were inside the house. The furniture was old and nearly worn out, the rugs scuffed and drab. But everything was spotlessly clean. They sat round a table with mugs of tea. Sharon was looking at the man now, her father. He was tall and slim with soft brown eyes and a strong, kindly face.

'I never wanted to give you away,' Iris said. Her

voice was much like Angie's, though softer. 'But my mother forced me to. All these years your dad and me have wondered about you. Wondered where you were, if you were happy . . .'

'People have been hard on us,' Reg said. 'Because we're poor, and because they know your mum gave you away to strangers, they think badly of us.' His hand closed gently over Sharon's. 'We're not bad people. We try our best.'

'Everything'll be all right now,' Sharon told him. 'We're together, that's what matters. We'll show everybody.' She looked at her mother. 'We'll make a go of things. Together.'

She woke up with the dampness of tears on her face. For a minute she lay and stared at the ceiling, recalling her mother's wistful, pretty face and the calm strength of her father.

She looked at the clock.

'Blast!'

It was after nine o'clock. They hadn't called her. She rolled out of bed, muttering under her breath, and trotted to the bathroom.

When she had bathed and brushed her teeth she stood in front of her open wardrobe and tried to decide which image she would present to the world today. After a minute she took out a pair of stone-washed jeans and a plain pink blouse. She completed the outfit with a white cotton windcheater, white socks and pink trainers. Dressed like that, she believed, anybody could be anybody.

As she went down the stairs, patting her hip pocket to make sure, for the third time, that she was carrying money, she heard Den and Angie arguing in the bar. Some things never change, Sharon thought.

The rasp of Angie's accusation hit the air as Sharon entered the bar. 'Den, you'd lie to me even if the truth sounded better!'

'I'm tellin' you the truth!' Den yelled back. 'I was down that garage till ten last night tryin' to get me car back. They'd lost a part, so I had to hang on.'

'Since when do mechanics work till that time of night?'

'Mornin',' Sharon said, glaring at them. 'It does a girl good to walk in on all this wedded bliss.'

Angie glared back at her, but Den suddenly looked sheepish. 'Sorry, Princess.' He glared at Angie. 'I guess we were makin' a bit too much out of nothin'.'

'You can call it nothin' if you want!' Angie shouted. 'But I know different.' She turned and stamped towards the ladies loo, hugging a box of cleaning materials.

Den shrugged at Sharon. 'I think with Ethel bein' off sick, an' your mum havin' to do all the cleaning' – well, it's makin' her temper a bit ragged.'

'The way you carry on doesn't help,' Sharon said. 'She wasn't bawlin' about havin' to clean the place just then, was she?'

Den didn't seem prepared to defend himself. He sighed quietly and leaned on the back shelf. 'You're right, I suppose.' He folded his arms and stared at Sharon. 'Would you believe I don't *try* to upset your mum? Or you? I don't want to upset anybody.'

Sharon remembered the dream: *We're not bad people. We try our best.*

'I'm gettin' a bit fed up with myself, Sharon.' For once he didn't appear to be putting up a cover. 'It dawned on me late last night. I'm supposed to be on top of things – a good businessman, good husband, capable father. But there's times I realize I'm about as much use as an ashtray on a motorbike.'

Against her will, Sharon felt a pang of sympathy for him. Stripped of the flash front, Den Watts could be a nice, fallible man.

'I could make things a lot better than they are, Princess. I know I could. There's lots I could have done already . . .

'Like stayin' in last night,' Sharon said, even though she didn't want to say it.

'I'll tell you somethin'. I *was* at the garage last night. Old Duffy worked late specially for me. Your mum won't believe that, of course . . .'

'Because you've lied to her so often before.' Sharon turned to the door sharply. She didn't want to go into it all again. Things didn't change. Den never would, that was for sure. 'I'll see you later.'

'Where are you goin'?'

'To see a couple of friends. I'll get somethin' to eat in a burger bar or somewhere.' Sharon glanced at Den once, quickly, as she opened the door. He looked so downcast she could have crossed and hugged him, but she pushed that urge aside. She wished Den and Angie wouldn't make her feel so sorry for them, sometimes.

Bright Lane didn't live up to its name. It was a short row of gnarled buildings with crumbly stone-work and the roofs patched, here and there, with sheets of tin. The George, a green-painted public house with ancient, dirty etched-glass windows and a solitary door, stood on the corner next to an Indian supermarket.

Sharon entered the bar a few minutes after opening time. There were three people there already; the landlord, who was so fat she wondered how he could reach the pumps, a man with several days' stubble on his chin and red-rimmed eyes, and an old woman, who sat in a corner and appeared to be whispering to her glass of stout.

The landlord waddled along the bar and nodded at Sharon. 'Yes, love?'

'Can I have a Coke, please?' She was doing her best to look and sound older, in case he objected to serving borderline minors.

'I can give you somethin' quite like a Coke. It's called Cola Fizz.'

Sharon hated the stuff. 'That'll be fine, thanks.'

Outside the tube station she had bought a newspaper, so she would have somewhere to rest her eyes while she waited in the pub. As the drink was put before her she folded the paper open to the women's page and stared at it without reading.

Four more customers came in during the next fifteen minutes. As Sharon glanced at each one her impression of the pub hardened. It was a loser's place, just like Lampton Close. The people who used The George had the hapless look of refugees, worn down by a life they couldn't understand. Whether that was their fault or not, she didn't know.

She couldn't make the drink last longer than

twenty minutes. Swallowing the last sickly mouthful, she asked the landlord for an orange juice.

So far, she thought, sipping the new drink, things weren't working out the way she had imagined. She supposed she'd been silly to expect her father to walk in, just like that, and be identified by name. It was possible he only used the place at night, like a lot of Den's customers. Or maybe only a couple of times a week. Or only at weekends. So far, anyway, nobody by the name of Reg had appeared.

Sharon decided to put Plan B into action. When the landlord was at her end of the bar again she asked him if Reg Porter had been in lately.

He shook his head. 'Lookin' for him, are you?'

'Yes. I was told he came in here.' A man who had been studying the racing page of his paper was now staring at Sharon. She pretended not to notice. 'I don't suppose you know where he and his wife live, do you?'

'No idea,' the landlord said. 'Do they owe you money?'

'Oh, no, nothing like that. I'm a relative.'

The man with the paper came along the bar and put his beer glass down beside Sharon. The landlord moved away. 'You're related to Reg Porter, eh?'

Sharon didn't like the look of him. He had a mean, thin-lipped mouth and lifeless grey eyes. His hands looked as if they had been badly modelled from blotchy yellow-brown plasticine. But perhaps he could tell her something. Sharon smiled at him brightly. 'That's right,' she said. 'Are you a friend of his?'

'A friend?' The man looked as if he had been

insulted. 'Garbage like that don't have friends.' He took a gulp from his glass, keeping his eyes on Sharon. 'You don't look to me like you could be related to the likes of him an' her.'

And you don't look like you could be related to anything outside a menagerie, Sharon thought. This was another low-lifer with bad opinions of everything and everybody. Sharon believed he was drunk, even though it was early.

She sidled away until she couldn't quite smell the man's breath. 'I'm related, all right.'

'Then I'm sorry for you.'

The landlord cleared his throat noisily, warning the man to behave.

'Do you know what that Reg Porter did, right here in this pub?' The man shook his head at the memory of it. 'He talked an old man out of his pension money. Good old Reg conned Bill, a harmless, silly old bloke, into thinkin' he was goin' to be back in an hour with the money.'

'Why would Reg do that?' Sharon demanded.

'He said he had to get a nightie an' some other stuff because his wife was goin' into hospital that mornin', an' the banks weren't open yet.' The man shook his head again. 'Old Bill's too thick to know the banks open before the pubs. He's too dumb to know a bank wouldn't let the likes of Reg Porter past the door, either.'

'That's enough,' the landlord said.

'I'm just lettin' this young woman know the kind of relations she's got.' The man wiped his mouth with his sleeve and took out a battered cigarette packet. 'There's nothin' rotten that Reg hasn't done.

75

Nothin' at all.' He lit a cigarette and blew smoke at the floor. 'An' as for that missus of his – a more drunken, thievin', foul-mouthed witch I've never – '

'Oi!' The landlord came forward. 'You can come in here an' drink any time you like,' he told the man, 'but I'll not have you startin' anythin'.'

The man looked indignant. 'The girl ought to know, right? You can see she's a decent type. She don't want to go dirtyin' herself gettin' near them two.'

'It's none of my business an' it's none of yours either,' the landlord said. 'Pack it in. Drink your beer an' study the horses. It's what you're best at.'

The man looked hard at Sharon for a moment, then he sighed and moved back along the bar, taking his drink with him. The landlord waited a few seconds, then came to Sharon's corner and leaned close.

'I'm sorry if he upset you, love.'

'He didn't upset me,' Sharon said. 'He doesn't know what he's talkin' about. He's drunk.'

'Yeah, you're right about him bein' drunk. He has a drink before he gets out of bed of a mornin'. But I think maybe he does know what he's talkin' about. He doesn't miss much, an' neither do I.'

They're all low-lifers, Sharon thought. The landlord included. She had heard rough characters in the Vic say things about other people that were just plain lies. It happened all the time.

'If you're lookin' for the Porters,' the landlord murmured, moving even closer and putting a terrible strain on his fat belly, 'you won't find them round here. They left the district about a month back. They had to.'

Trying to keep the resentment and disappointment out of her voice, Sharon said, 'Have you any idea where they went?'

'Well, there's so much rumour flies about in a pub, it's hard to sort out the fact from the fancy, love. But I heard they'd moved to Walford.'

Sharon forgot her resentment. Disappointment faded, too. 'Walford? Do you know where, exactly?'

'No idea. But I think it's genuine information, as far as it goes – I was earwiggin' a conversation between two lads that know Reg.' He paused. 'Two *bad* lads, I might say.'

Walford, Sharon was thinking. All the time and effort she had spent, and they were on her own doorstep! If ever there was an omen, though, this was it. What more powerful hint could fate throw at her? She was meant to find them, it was the clearest kind of destiny.

She emptied her glass and thanked the landlord.

'You take care,' he said, sounding as if he really meant it.

Out on the street Sharon paused, fighting down the memory of what had been said about her parents. She had often heard things about Den and Angie that just couldn't have been true, yet people believed the tales with no resistance at all. That was the way people were. Somewhere in Walford she had two poor, put-upon parents who were struggling along the best way they could. It was only natural they would be picked on. It was human nature to keep stepping on the downtrodden.

The dream came drifting back. *We're not bad people. We try our best*. That was the thought to hold. Sharon would hold it tightly, until the search was over and she could see for herself that the dream was true.

8

There was probably nothing Rob Garnett wouldn't do for Sharon. The trouble was, she hadn't let him do a single thing for her so far. She wasn't even rude to him, in fact she was always pleasant when he spoke to her, but Rob felt Sharon was careful never to let the distance between them get any narrower.

That didn't deter him. Rob believed in holding on to his dreams until they came true. He was nineteen and personable, a young man with ambition. The way he saw it, the future was his. He had made several decisions to guarantee his place in the world.

'I'm a go-getter,' he had once told Sharon proudly. 'I know where I'm goin'. There's not many can say that.'

He would start his own stall when he had saved enough from working on his dad's. Sheets, duvets, pillows and pillowcases were always in demand; he knew all the cut-price suppliers and out-of-town manufacturers as well as his father did, so he could run an efficient, profitable business. That plan would see to his security.

Another plan was to get his own place, just as soon as he could. It would be a nice modern flat, not too big. He would furnish it by stages, buying only the best and only when he could properly afford it. That way, he would have a nice pad to go home to at night, but he wouldn't put himself in debt for it, the way some mugs did.

The other major plan was to marry the girl of his dreams, so that when he went home after a hard day's slog she would be there, waiting for him, welcoming him with open arms. Nobody else but Sharon Watts could fill the bill. Therefore, Sharon it had to be. Rob was prepared to bide his time. In the meantime, he'd do what he could to let Sharon see how right he was for her.

On Thursday morning, as he was setting out the latest selection of floral duvet covers on his dad's stall, his spirits lifted a mega-notch as he turned and saw Sharon standing on the pavement two metres away, staring at him. She looked very thoughtful, as if something had just occurred to her. Which it had.

'Mornin', Sharon.' Rob gave her his confident, welcoming grin. He touched his hair swiftly to make sure his George Michael quiff was still in place. 'Come to brighten me day, have you?'

Sharon lost her distant expression and smiled at him. 'It's bright enough, I should have thought.'

'Boilin', intit? Still, things always get sunnier when you show up.'

'Bet you say that to all the girls.'

'Nah.' Rob came round the stall and leaned on the edge. 'I'm careful with the compliments, Sharon. I save them all for you.'

For Sharon, talking to Rob was like wading against a stream. It was never two-way, never casual. He was always bombarding her with flattery and sales chats about his own talent. She knew some lads of fourteen who could teach Rob a thing or two about coming on cool.

'I was wonderin' if you could do me a favour, Rob.'

His face tightened with pleasure. She had never asked a single thing of him before. Patience was paying off. 'It'd be a pleasure. An' if I can't do it for you, nobody can.'

'It's somebody I'm lookin' for,' Sharon explained. 'It's not me that's lookin' for him, actually, it's this friend, but I promised I'd help. It's a relative of hers that she wants to get in touch with.'

Rob had developed a tiny frown. 'Has she a rough idea where he might be? I mean, London's a big place.'

'Oh, he's here in Walford. She knows that. But Walford's pretty big, too. I know you use quite a few different pubs, so I thought if maybe you could ask around . . .'

'Certainly. No sweat. What's the bloke's name?'

'Reg Porter. He's got a wife called Iris.'

'I'll make enquiries,' Rob said. 'I'm pretty good at findin' what other people can't. I've got a talent for it.'

Sharon nodded, as if she had never doubted that. 'It's a surprise my friend's got for him, so the sooner he's located, the better.'

'I get the message.' Rob stood away from the stall sharply and put his hands on his hips. He gave Sharon his big confident grin again, showing her just what a positive hunk he was. 'Fancy havin' a bit of Chinese with me on Saturday? Then we could maybe go on to a disco.'

Sharon found herself acting again. She didn't want to seem like she was rebuffing him. 'Aw, isn't that just typical?' She frowned along the road at The Vic.

'What's up?'

Sharon sighed. 'The first Saturday in ages I get a chance to go somewhere, I've gone an' promised Mum an' Dad I'd help out in the pub.'

'Well, couldn't you cry off?'

Sharon made a reluctant face. 'I'm a bit like you in that department, Rob. A promise is a promise.'

He nodded, understanding. 'It can be tough, havin' principles. How about next week?'

'That'd be nice. If it's all right with my folks, of course . . .'

'They can rely on me, Sharon,' Rob said, his face turning serious. 'I know how to respect a girl an' look after her.'

Sharon fluttered her eyelashes. 'I'm sure you do.' She felt she had smoothed over that ripple nicely and got right back to business. 'You'll ask around meantime then, will you?'

'Stand on me, Sharon. Reg Porter's this geezer's name, right? If he's around, I'll find him.'

As Sharon walked away from the stall she smothered a little pang of guilt. Rob was such a pushover. It wouldn't even occur to him she was cashing-in on the fact he fancied her so strongly. On the other hand, it wasn't too big-headed to reckon she'd made his day.

'I think the emergency's over,' Angie told Den as Sharon came into the pub and went upstairs.

Den gave a customer his change. 'I never thought

82

there was an emergency in the first place, did I?' He wiped his fingers on a towel. 'What makes you think things have changed?'

'She's stickin' close to home, like she used to. An' she's not so edgy.'

Den spread his hands. 'See? It was a phase, that's all it was. Just one of the countless waves on the tide of youth.'

'Very poetic,' Angie grunted. 'I'm dead relieved, I can tell you. For a time there I thought she was plannin' to take off.'

'Not a chance of it,' Den said flatly. 'She might moan an' mope a bit, but this is where her heart is.' He paused. 'I was thinkin' of gettin' her a little present.'

Angie blinked at him. 'What kind of little present?'

'Oh, I thought a watch, maybe. Somethin' with a bit of quality.'

'What for?'

He shrugged. 'To make up for one or two things. I can see a lot of it gets on top of her – you an' me havin' the odd ding-dong, not spendin' enough time with her – things like that.'

Angie smiled. 'You're really just a big softie, aren't you?' She poked his ribs. 'All brittle shell, but marshmallow inside.'

Den nodded, straight faced. 'Of course I am. Ask anybody.'

Upstairs, Sharon was making her second set of telephone calls on the kitchen extension. Before she had gone out for a break – and had the sudden idea of getting Rob Garnett to do some snooping for her

– she had called eight pubs in Walford and spoken to the landlords. To each of them she identified herself as Miss Teale, of the solicitors' firm Watts, Fowler and Beale. Miss Teale was the name of one of Sharon's teachers, and on the 'phone she tried to impersonate the woman's vinegary voice. The landlords all received the same request:

'I'm making enquiries about a Mr Reginald Porter, who lives in your area. I believe he's known familiarly as Reg. Mr Porter's been mentioned in a client's will and we're anxious to trace him. Does anyone of that name use your public house?'

So far, no one Sharon spoke to had heard of Reg. The list of Walford pubs she'd put together was as daunting, in its way, as the electoral rolls she had ploughed through over in Islington. Each call took a minimum twenty-five seconds. On top of that, it took ten seconds to dial and often as long as fifteen seconds before the receiver at the other end was picked up. That meant each call took roughly a minute, and there were another fifty-three pubs on the list. It was a lot to get through with no guarantee of success. But Sharon still figured it was the best way to trace Reg. If it failed, she would have to think of something else.

At twenty-past twelve, delivering her speech to the landlord of The Vine on Carver Road, she decided that she would break for a cup of coffee after this call. Her throat was beginning to hurt.

'He's been mentioned in a client's will and we're anxious to trace him. Does anyone of that name use – '

'Reg Porter, you say?' the landlord cut in. 'He

comes in here, yeah. Every night since he moved to the district.'

Sharon was speechless for a moment. She had been ready to drop the receiver as soon as the man said he didn't know any Reg Porter.

'Hello? Miss Whatsit? You still there?'

'Yes, yes, I'm still here.' What would she say now? 'Will Mr Porter be there tonight?' And if so, she thought frantically, *what*?

'I'm pretty sure he will be, yeah. Shall I tell him you called?'

'Ah . . .' Her mind suddenly clicked back on to the rails. 'Would you happen to know his address?'

''Fraid not, love. All I know is he's in digs somewhere round here.'

'Well, in that case,' Sharon said, 'we'll send one of our employees round to your place tonight. Perhaps if you'd point out Mr Porter to her, she can carry out the formalities there and save him the trouble of calling on us.'

'Right, love.'

'And I think it would be nice if this is a surprise for Mr Porter, so if you wouldn't mention this call . . .'

'I get the message,' the landlord assured her. 'Mum's the word.' He chuckled throatily. 'We'll be seein' your lady later on then.'

'Yes, indeed. Thank you for your help.'

As she hung up the telephone Angie came into the kitchen. She looked at the lists of scribbled addresses on the table. 'What's all this stuff, darlin'?'

'It's a project for school,' Sharon said, flustered.

She snatched up the papers before Angie could see the names of all those pubs.

'Got you workin' in the holidays now, have they?'

'That's right.' Sharon moved to the door.

'Are things OK now?' Angie was looking at her with her soft, dewy eyes. 'I mean, there's nothin' troublin' you?'

'Of course there isn't. You imagine things, Mum.'

'Yeah, I suppose I do,' Angie murmured, watching as Sharon went off to her bedroom.

She walked into The Vine at eight-thirty, dressed the way she imagined a solicitors' employee might look. Her round-necked black jumper, black pencil skirt and black high heels contrasted nicely with her candy-striped cotton jacket, creating an impression of after-hours formality.

She was relieved to find The Vine was a bright, cheerful place with a nice carpet, polished fittings and a decent jukebox. There was a good mix of age groups, too. Sharon took a stool at the bar between two chattering trios of young people. She smiled at the tall man with the neatly trimmed white moustache as he came along the bar from serving another customer.

'Are you the landlord?' she asked him.

'That's me. Tom Tucker at your service – an' yes, I sometimes sing for me supper, before you ask.' He leaned forward, lowering his voice. 'You wouldn't be the young lady from the solicitors, would you?'

'That's right.'

Tucker winked. 'I thought you were. You look the part, somehow.'

Sharon was flattered. Maybe she should take up impersonation as a full-time job. 'Is Mr Porter here yet?'

'Not yet, no. He comes in nearer nine o'clock, sometimes a bit earlier. Fancy a drink while you're waitin'?'

Sharon asked for a Coke and got a real one this time. She sipped it slowly, looking round the room, enjoying the steady beat of the music. It seemed to have been a long trail that had led to this moment. Even so, she was glad the meeting would take place in these friendly, civilized surroundings. As the minutes ticked past her excitement began to mount, as it had before. But behind it Sharon felt a hard prop of self-assurance. She wasn't quite the giddy, unprepared girl she'd been at the beginning of the search.

'On your own, then?'

Sharon turned and saw a young man standing by her stool. He was squat, oily-skinned and pimply. What's this strange power I have over slobs? she wondered.

'I'm waitin' for somebody.'

'Anybody in particular?'

'My boyfriend,' Sharon snapped.

'Maybe he's decided not to come.' He smiled. It reminded Sharon of the way some people looked when they were about to throw up.

'He'll be here.'

The youth didn't budge. 'Maybe I know him. From round here, is he?'

Sharon stared at him. 'Yeah, he is. Maybe you do

know him. He's about six-foot four, does body-buildin', an' he's as bad tempered as a scrap dealer's dog.'

The young man made an attempt at a scornful sneer, but he moved away, anyway.

Sharon gulped down more Coke and looked at the clock. It wouldn't be long now. This was threshold time, the toughest part to endure. She drained the glass and turned to ask for another drink. As she did the landlord was coming towards her.

'He's here,' he said excitedly. 'Just came in.'

Sharon's eyes searched the group of people at the corner of the bar where Tom Tucker had pointed. 'Where?' she said, her heart pounding. 'Which one?'

'Him in the green sweater.'

She blinked a couple of times. Green sweater. She couldn't see anybody with a green sweater. She scanned the group again, then she saw him.

'Thanks,' she said to the landlord as he moved away. She got off the stool and walked to the end of the bar. When she was sure the landlord wasn't watching, she slipped out on to the street and leaned on the wall by the door.

'You dope,' she told herself.

She should have known better than build up her hopes that way. If she'd been a lot less certain tonight was the night, she wouldn't be feeling so crushed now.

'Bubble-head!'

There had to be more than one Reg Porter in Walford, after all. There were probably dozens. The man Tom Tucker pointed out was one of them, Sharon didn't doubt it for a minute. But he wasn't the one she was looking for. Not unless it was possible for a black man of about twenty to have a sixteen-year-old daughter with blonde hair and blue eyes.

9

Ethel was back at work, trotting round the pub with her dusters and polish, followed by her pug dog, Willie. Sharon wasn't sure what Ethel was singing, but it grated on her eardrums. She waited until the old woman had gone upstairs before she lifted the telephone and dialled the number of the Social Services Department at the Walford Council Offices.

The number was ringing out when Den appeared at her side. Sharon put down the 'phone.

'Engaged,' she muttered, glancing at Den's grinning face. 'What's so funny, then?'

'One of the draymen told me a joke.'

She could see he wanted to pass it on. 'Go on, then.'

'What goes "clip"?'

'I don't know.'

'A one-legged horse.'

Sharon groaned. 'That's pathetic.'

'Well . . .' Den shrugged. 'It don't take much to amuse an old man like me.'

'If you're an old man, what does that make me?' Angie demanded from the top of the stairs. She came hobbling down, gripping the banister, miming old age. 'I'm three years older than you, Sunshine.'

'Ah,' Den said, 'but you're one of them ageless types, aren't you, Duchess?'

Amazing, Sharon thought. They were calling one

another "Sunshine" and "Duchess". They were actually being friendly and good-natured towards each other.

'Did you get all the beer you ordered?' Angie asked, pausing in the doorway to the bar. 'No clangers this time? No barrels of lager where you wanted bitter, or bottles of barley wine where you asked for Guinness?'

'Everythin' spot on,' Den said. 'In fact, since I got up this mornin', nothin's gone wrong. I can hardly believe it.' He turned and gave Sharon a squeeze. 'Fancy makin' your old dad a cup of coffee, Princess? I feel like sittin' down in the bar for a while an' wallowin' in my good luck, before everythin' turns sour again.'

'An' one for your decrepit mum an' all, love,' Angie said. 'I'm spittin' feathers.'

An instant before she went up to the kitchen, Sharon saw Den give Angie a gentle pat on the shoulder.

Closing the kitchen door to muffle the sound of Ethel's singing, Sharon filled the kettle and switched it on. Den and Angie were such a puzzle, she thought. For all their squabbling and up-front hostility, they were held together by some bond, a strong one, that had nothing to do with harmony. Maybe they both needed strife in their lives. Perhaps that was what united them, a need for regular warfare.

This morning's truce between them unsettled Sharon, somehow. It was so much easier to carry on her quest against a background of chaos and insecurity. She felt like a traitor, tracking down her real parents while Den and Angie, all unaware, went happily about their lives.

'It won't last,' she reminded herself aloud. She spooned instant coffee into the cups, hoping she could get some privacy soon to make that 'phone call.

Her opportunity came soon after opening time. There was the usual Friday-morning rush and both Den and Angie had to stay behind the bar to cope with the orders. Sharon helped them for a while, then said she had to go upstairs for a few minutes. She shut herself in the kitchen and dialled Social Services again.

'Ah, hello,' she said sharply to the switchboard girl. This time her voice was low and businesslike. 'Can I speak to somebody who deals with welfare claims?'

The line went dead for a minute, then a man's voice came on the line. He asked if he could help.

'I hope so. I'm with the Inland Revenue – the office of the Inspector of Taxes, actually.' She had read it on the front of a brown envelope lying beside the toaster. 'We're checking on the affairs of a couple in the Walford area, and I was wondering if I could have some details of their welfare claims.' It wasn't such a long shot, she believed. Reg and Iris were hard up, and people in their plight were likely to be on the books of the Social Services. 'The name's Porter, Reginald and Iris Porter.'

'Are they in some kind of trouble with the tax, then?' the man asked.

'Oh no, far from it. They may be due a refund, actually.'

'I see. Can you give me their address?'

'Well no,' Sharon said smoothly. 'That's a problem we hoped you could help us with. We have information that they're in the Walford area, but we've no idea where.'

Now the man's voice became guarded. 'You know the security difficulties we have, passing information by phone from one official department to another . . .'

'Of course.' Sharon had no idea what he meant.

'We get private detectives and debt collectors calling us up, claiming to be the tax, or the police, just to get hold of an address.'

Sharon swallowed softly. 'Of course, we get the same difficulty here . . .'

'So, if you don't mind, we'll play this the safe way.'

'Pardon?'

'I'll call you back at the tax office. OK?'

'Certainly.'

'If you'll just give me your name and department, then.'

Sharon hit the button and slammed the receiver on the hook. 'Blast!' she hissed. 'Blast, *blast*!'

Angie came dashing in carrying an empty ice bucket. 'Some people put enough ice in their drinks to sink the Titanic.' She jerked open the fridge and pulled out one of the ice trays. Then she noticed Sharon's scowl. 'What's the matter, love?'

'Nothin'.'

'It don't look like nothin'. Has somethin' upset you?'

'No.' Sharon made for the door. 'I'm just in a mood. It'll pass.'

'Well, there's a nice-lookin' young fella down in the bar askin' for you. Maybe that'll cheer you up.'

Sharon sighed and went downstairs. As she entered the bar she saw Rob Garnett smiling at her.

'Hi there,' he said, over-brightly.

'Hi.' It was a bit soon to ask him if he'd had any luck, Sharon thought, but she asked him anyway.

'Yup,' Rob said. 'I've found the bloke you're lookin' for. Well, I've near enough found him, anyway.'

Sharon was suddenly all ears. 'You want a drink while you tell me?'

'Never touch it in daylight, Sharon. That's a mug's game. But maybe I'll have a lemonade, just to be sociable.'

Sharon jerked the tops off two lemonade bottles and grabbed a couple of glasses. 'Over here,' she said, pointing to a corner seat. 'I don't want anybody listenin' in.' They sat down and Sharon poured the drinks.

'Maybe it was luck,' Rob said, after a slow, thoughtful sip from his glass. 'But I wouldn't be too sure about that.' He made a lopsided smile. 'When I go out deliberately to do somethin', I reckon I set up a magnetic field. I can sort of home-in on what I'm after.'

Sharon nodded, trying to hold down her impatience.

'You don't come across that kind of thing often, Sharon. A guy goes out with one purpose in mind

94

and before you know it, he's hit the jackpot. It's a built-in gift, I suppose.'

'So what happened?'

'Oh, I was in The Plough last night. Third place I'd visited. Durin' the evenin' I'd asked maybe twenty people if they knew a Reg Porter. Nobody did. Then I was givin' this guy a light for his fag an' I thought, why not ask him, in passin', like. So as soon as I mention the name he looks interested. He asks who's lookin' for Reg. I explained an' he nodded. "I know him," he says. "In fact, he's a mate of mine." So I got talkin', just to see how much I could pick up for you.'

Sharon held her excitement in check. It could be the wrong Reg Porter again.

'The man you're lookin' for seems to be a bit dodgy, Sharon. I got the impression he's lyin' low.'

'How did you get that impression?'

'Well, his mate wouldn't give me an address. Said he could pass on any messages. He told me Reg doesn't go out these days.'

'Can I talk to this man?'

Rob nodded. 'He'll be in The Plough at one o'clock today. His name's Fred Lockwood. You can't miss him, actually. He looks like somethin' off Spittin' Image – big rubbery lips, nostrils the size of sunglasses, spiky red hair an' a terrible smoker's cough. He drinks pints of snakebite an' seems to have a season ticket for the table beside the fireplace.'

Sharon nodded. He certainly wouldn't be hard to spot from that description. But was he the friend of the right Reg Porter?

'Did he say much about Reg?'

'Not really,' Rob said. 'He did confirm the wife's name is Iris, though.'

Now it all looked different to Sharon. 'Rob, you're a pal.' she said.

'You better believe it,' he murmured, trying to put a lot of meaning into his voice. 'Any time I can help, you only have to ask.'

Sharon finished her drink and pushed back her stool. 'I better get movin' if I've to be over at The Plough by one.'

'No rush, Sharon. Fred Lockwood looks the type that'll hang around till closin' time.'

'Even so,' Sharon said, standing. 'I'm anxious to get this over an' done with.'

Rob looked disappointed. 'I got my Dad to let me have an hour off. What am I goin' to do with the rest of the time?'

'Have another drink on me, then sit there an' figure out what we're goin' to eat next Saturday.' Sharon could see that pleased him. Whatever the outcome of her meeting with Fred Lockwood, she would let Rob take her out next week, anyway. She just hoped she wouldn't fall asleep in the middle of dinner.

The Plough was jammed to the doors. The workers from two nearby factories finished at noon on a Friday. Sharon had the feeling most of them were packed into the two bars, jostling, shouting, laughing and swallowing gallons of beer. She fought her way to the bar and asked the barmaid for a tonic water. Holding it with both hands, she struggled to the fringe of the crowd and looked around.

The table by the fireside was deserted, as they all were. This crowd liked to stand. Sharon looked at the clock. It was five past one. More waiting, she thought glumly, then saw a man in a rust-coloured jacket shuffling along close to the wall, clutching a pint of cloudy yellow liquid which was unmistakably snakebite. He fitted Rob's description, too. He looked like he had been made as a joke.

Sharon waited until he sat down at the fireside table, then she went across.

'Excuse me. Are you Fred Lockwood?'

'Yeah.' He said it defiantly. 'So what?'

Sharon explained she was the girl he had been told about, the one looking for Reg Porter.

The thick lips rubbed slowly across each other as he looked her up and down.

'My name's Sharon,' she said, trying to make herself sound open and trustworthy. 'Can I sit down?'

Fred hesitated, then nodded. 'How come you're so keen to get in touch with Reg?'

Sharon settled in her chair and put the glass in front of her. 'He's a relative. I only found out recently, but now I'm dyin' to meet him. And Iris.'

'Didn't know Reg had any relatives.' It was said in a way that suggested Fred had a tiny doubt about Sharon. But only a tiny one.

'I've been huntin' everywhere for them. Bethnal Green, Islington, now Walford.'

'You've been followin' the right route, sure enough.' All at once Fred seemed to relax. 'An'

97

you don't look like you're the type to mean Reg an' Iris any harm.'

'God, no,' Sharon said emphatically. 'I just want to meet them. An' help them, if I can.'

Fred sighed, making his huge nostrils flare. 'It's a shame about Reg, the luck he's had. He could certainly use some help.'

'Have you known him long?'

Fred nodded. 'Years. I met him inside.' He narrowed his eyes. 'You know about him bein' inside, do you? I don't want to go spreadin' no stories he wouldn't want me to.'

'I – I'd heard there'd been some trouble, yeah.'

'It's the system, love.' Fred took a gulp from his pint, then wiped the surplus from his lips with a tongue the colour of a doormat. 'If they're against you, they stay against you. Fred only took the money because he wanted to get some grub. A man's got to eat, hasn't he? If the system don't give you no money, there's nothin' to do but help yourself. Stands to reason.'

'Of course,' Sharon forced herself to say.

'An' the other business, when he broke up the fight between Iris an' the policewoman – that was the system workin' against them again. It was his elbow that caught the female bobby in the jaw. A simple accident, but they done him for it.'

'Why was Iris fightin' with a policewoman?'

Fred shrugged. 'It was just a case of one thing leadin' to another. A shopkeeper accused Iris of nickin' somethin'. Well, she'd had a bit to drink, so she most likely made a mistake. Anyway, she lands

98

one on the shopkeeper's chin, because the swine had insulted her, an' one thing led to another . . .'

'Oh. I see.' This was beginning to depress Sharon.

'They've never had much luck, far as I can tell. People are too ready to point the finger at them, without givin' the couple a chance. I know it's true that maybe they drink a bit too much, but booze is their solace, intit? I mean *you'd* be drunk most of the time if the whole world was against you, right?'

It occurred to Sharon, almost as a wistful hope, that Fred Lockwood could be talking about another Reg and Iris Porter. 'Did you know they had a baby at one time?'

Fred nodded. 'Fifteen, sixteen years back, somethin' like that. Reg told me about it in the nick. We had plenty of time to talk in there. It was a girl, as I remember. They got it adopted, didn't they?'

Sharon nodded.

'Yeah, well, best thing, I suppose. I mean Iris is a good sort in my book, but she's not the kind to have kids. A woman what likes a drink an' a knees-up can't do with bein' tied at home with a kid.'

Sharon felt something was being taken from her. 'How old is Iris?' she asked.

'Oh, about forty, I'd say. She manages to look a bit younger, though. She keeps her hair bleached an' done up in a beehive, you know? An' she still wears mini-skirts an' the old stilettoes. She's a lively girl, is Iris.' Fred grinned, revealing tombstone teeth. 'I'm glad they came to stay in Walford. As a matter of fact I got them the digs, right round the corner from where I stay.'

'Don't they go out much these days?'

Fred frowned at his glass before he took another gulp. 'They can't, love. DHSS is lookin' for them. Some pen-pusher found out they was collectin' more benefit than they're allowed. Usin' two sets of names an' addresses, see.' He sniffed. 'Folk do it all the time. They *need* to, just to get enough to live on. But that's Reg an' Iris's luck all over. They got caught, or nearly. They legged it out of the office double quick. The DHSS don't know their real address, so they're keepin' indoors until the heat dies down.'

Sharon didn't want to hear any more. 'Can you let me have their address? I promise you I don't mean them any harm.'

'I can tell you don't, love. I've no worries on that score. They're at number 18 Mercer Road. Livin' under the name of Stewart, for the time bein'.'

'Thanks,' Sharon said, memorizing the address. She looked at her drink and decided to leave it. She stood up.

'I haven't been round to see them for a couple of days,' Fred said, 'so give them my best, eh? When I get my Giro I'll take round a couple of cans of beer. Tell them that. It'll cheer them up.'

Sharon promised she would pass on the message, and she told Fred she would leave the price of a pint behind the bar for him. She thanked him again and left.

For a minute she stood on the pavement, gazing in the direction of Mercer Road. It was only two turnings away. At her usual speed she could be there in three minutes.

She sighed and began walking back to Albert Square. There was too much churning in her head, too much making her ache. She would need time to let it all settle before she made up her mind.

10

When she got home she went to her room, closed the door softly and sat on the bed. She had never felt so unprotected. Looking round at her things – clothes, books, the piles of cassette tapes and the posters on the walls – she realized that this place mirrored exactly who she was. The personality of Sharon Watts was stamped on her room. In spite of all the faces she could hide behind, the disguises she could use to fool the world outside, the room told the truth. Sharon was a mixed-up teenage girl, discontented, resentful, badly in need of something solid to support her.

And now she began to wonder if she had been getting things wrong all along. She had looked outside for her solid ground. She had tried to find it with boys, with money and music and countless other things; they had let her down, she had still felt she was adrift. Tracking down her real parents had seemed like the perfect answer. Knowing who they were, she'd believed, would give her a proper sense of who she was and where she stood.

Something was telling her now that she had to look *inside* for her strength and support. The notion wasn't very clear, but it was there and it wouldn't budge.

'What'll I do?' she whispered.

She had to face the truth, for a start. She hadn't

heard one good word about her real mother and father. Even Fred Lockwood, the man who was their friend, had painted an awful picture. All the evidence led to one very clear conclusion; Reg and Iris Porter were terrible people. Sharon couldn't kid herself, not any more.

But they were her parents. She thought of the days of searching, the setbacks, the disappointments. Now she was past all that, she could go to where they lived and she could see them and talk to them. The urge to meet them was still there, defying common sense.

'It'd be a mistake,' she hissed to herself. But part of her wasn't listening, some small glimmer of unthinking hope wanted her to complete her mission.

Sharon lay back on the covers, waiting for her confusion to settle. Her mind began to drift. The tensions and frustrations of the past week had drained her. Within five minutes she was asleep.

She woke up in the late afternoon. Sitting up, she rubbed her eyes and looked round the silent room again. She couldn't remember dreaming, but something had been decided while she slept. For good or ill, she *had* to go and see Reg and Iris. They were her real mother and father, after all. There was no way she could deny herself that meeting.

As she entered the bar Den was sitting at one of the tables, working on the books.

'Hello, love,' he said, smiling warmly. 'Off out again, are you?'

'Just for a little while.'

Den stood up, fumbling in his jacket pocket. 'I

got you a little something.' He handed her a small oblong box covered in blue leather.

'What's this for?' Sharon turned it in her hands, reluctant to open it.

'Just a present,' Den said quietly. 'From Dad to his Princess.'

Sharon opened the box. It was a tiny, beautifully-made watch, with a gold case and bracelet and silver hands. 'It's lovely,' Sharon murmured, thinking *God! Why has he done this now, at this very time?*

'Sure you like it, darlin'?'

Sharon stood on tiptoe and kissed his cheek. 'I love it.' She knew if she stood there another second she would cry. She turned sharply and strode to the door, elbowing her way out as fast as she could.

Den stood watching the door as it swung shut. He would never admit it to Angie, but he had a sudden, strong feeling that something serious was happening for Sharon. He also felt, just as strongly, that no one should interfere.

An old woman opened the door and peered cautiously round the edge. 'Yes?'

'I've come to see Mr and Mrs Port – ah, I mean Stewart,' Sharon said.

'What's it about?' The woman showed a little more of her face as she examined Sharon carefully.

'I've a message for them.' When the woman didn't respond, Sharon added, 'It's to do with the Social Services, actually.' It couldn't hurt to put the hint of an official label on herself, she thought.

The woman hesitated, then she drew the door wide. 'You'd better come in.'

Sharon stepped into the musty hallway and waited as the woman closed the door again. There was a steep, narrow staircase at the far end of the hall. Her parents must live up there, Sharon thought.

'I'm Gladys Avery,' the woman announced. 'This house is mine. I let out four of the rooms as bedsits. I've been doin' it for over ten years. Until now I've never had any trouble with my tenants, nothin' serious, anyway.' She stepped past Sharon and pointed to the stairs 'If you'll follow me . . .'

They climbed to the first landing. Gladys paused by a chipped, brown-painted door and fished out a bunch of keys from her apron pocket. She located one key, put it in the lock and twisted it sharply. The door swung open.

'There,' she said. 'See for yourself.'

Sharon stepped into the room. The air was stale and thick with the smells of cooking. By the sink there was a pile of unwashed clothing. Dirty plates and pans were crammed in the wash bowl. The cooker was coated with grease.

Sharon turned and looked questioningly at Gladys.

'Just look at that bed, love. Can you imagine anybody sleepin' in that?'

The grimy sheets were in a tangle on the bare mattress. The pillows were smudged, as if someone had cleaned something with them.

Sharon looked at Gladys again. 'Is this – '

'This is where the Stewarts lived. They would never let me in. I can see why, now.'

Lived? Sharon thought. 'You mean they've left?'

'Two days ago,' Gladys said. 'They took the

105

money out of the gas meter with them.' She sighed. 'I've not been able to bring meself to come in an' clean the place. But I'll have to do it some time, I suppose.'

'Do you know where they went?'

'No idea,' Gladys said. 'They left some time durin' the night. About a week ago I heard him down in the hallway, tellin' her they'd best get out of London altogether. So where they skipped off to is anybody's guess.' She shook her head slowly, gazing round the filthy room. 'It's cost me, but thank the Lord I'm rid of them.'

As they went downstairs again Gladys launched into a catalogue of the hard time she'd had with her vanished tenants. 'They were always gettin' drunk, you know. He fell right down the stairs one night an' was too stewed to get on his feet again without help. When they wasn't up there boozin' an' fightin' with one another, they was stealin' stuff out of my kitchen cupboards. Whenever I complained they either ignored me or threatened me.'

Sharon looked at the frail old figure as they reached the hallway. 'They threatened you?'

'Her, that Iris, she told me she'd break my arm if I didn't stop moanin'. One day she got in a fight with one of me other tenants an' nearly *did* break her arm. To tell you the truth, I got that wary of them two I was scared to call in the Law, for fear of what they might come back an' do to me.'

Gladys shuffled to the front door and opened it. 'You've had a wasted journey, love. But I thought I'd best give you an idea of the sort of people you're lookin' for.'

'Thanks,' Sharon murmured as she stepped outside.

'They're not the sort a girl like you wants anythin' to do with. Nor anybody else, for that matter.'

Walking back home, Sharon felt relief spread through her. The trail had gone cold, and she had to admit she was glad. She had a perfect excuse to abandon the search for her parents, and she was taking it. All that effort, she thought, all that slogging, and this was what it came to.

But it hadn't been wasted, she decided as she paused and strapped on her new watch. There had been no waste at all. In looking for Reg and Iris she had found a better understanding of who she was. Earlier that day, she had felt she should look inside herself for the elusive solid ground. Now she believed it was within sight. She had learned how practical she could be, how patient and inventive. For the first time, she realized she had the strength to shape her life to suit her needs. All it took was hard work and no self-pity.

When she arrived at The Vic, Den and Angie were attending to last-minute jobs before opening time.

'Hello, you two,' Sharon said brightly. 'Fancy a cuppa while you're doin' that?'

Den and Angie looked at each other.

'That'd be smashin', darlin',' Angie said.

Den nodded. 'Spot on, kid.'

They looked at each other again as Sharon went upstairs, humming softly.

In the kitchen she took off her jacket, pushed up her sleeves and started getting a tea tray ready. She didn't want to figure out all the reasons why she felt so good. She just did, and she'd accept that.

Spooning tea into the pot, she realized that apart from everything else she'd learned, it had been a blessing just to find how fortunate she was.

'The jammiest girl in Walford,' she murmured.

She thought of Den and Angie and smiled. Whatever their failings and faults, they genuinely loved her. And she loved them. They were her folks, after all. They were the couple who'd cherished her since she came into their lives – and they were miles better than the folks she might have had, if she hadn't been so lucky.

Fiction in paperback from Dragon Books

Richard Dubleman
The Adventures of Holly Hobbie   £1.25 ☐

Anne Digby
Trebizon series
First Term at Trebizon   £1.50 ☐
Second Term at Trebizon   £1.50 ☐
Summer Term at Trebizon   £1.50 ☐
Boy Trouble at Trebizon   £1.50 ☐
More Trouble at Trebizon   £1.50 ☐
The Tennis Term at Trebizon   £1.50 ☐
Summer Camp at Trebizon   £1.50 ☐
Into the Fourth at Trebizon   £1.25 ☐
The Hockey Term at Trebizon   £1.50 ☐
The Big Swim of the Summer   60p ☐
A Horse Called September   £1.50 ☐
Me, Jill Robinson and the Television Quiz   £1.25 ☐
Me, Jill Robinson and the Seaside Mystery   £1.25 ☐
Me, Jill Robinson and the Christmas Pantomime   £1.25 ☐
Me, Jill Robinson and the School Camp Adventure   £1.25 ☐

Elyne Mitchell
Silver Brumby's Kingdom   85p ☐
Silver Brumbies of the South   95p ☐
Silver Brumby   85p ☐
Silver Brumby's Daughter   85p ☐
Silver Brumby Whirlwind   50p ☐

Mary O'Hara
My Friend Flicka Part One   85p ☐
My Friend Flicka Part Two   60p ☐

To order direct from the publisher just tick the titles you want
and fill in the order form.

Fiction in paperback from Dragon Books

Peter Glidewell
Schoolgirl Chums	£1.25	☐
St Ursula's in Danger	£1.25	☐
Miss Prosser's Passion	£1.50	☐

Enid Gibson
The Lady at 99	£1.50	☐

Gerald Frow
Young Sherlock: The Mystery of the Manor House	95p	☐
Young Sherlock: The Adventure at Ferryman's Creek	£1.50	☐

Frank Richards
Billy Bunter of Greyfriars School	£1.25	☐
Billy Bunter's Double	£1.25	☐
Billy Bunter Comes for Christmas	£1.25	☐
Billy Bunter Does His Best	£1.25	☐
Billy Bunter's Benefit	£1.50	☐
Billy Bunter's Postal Order	£1.50	☐

Dale Carlson
Jenny Dean Mysteries
Mystery of the Shining Children	£1.50	☐
Mystery of the Hidden Trap	£1.50	☐
Secret of the Third Eye	£1.50	☐

Marlene Fanta Shyer
My Brother the Thief	95p	☐

David Rees
The Exeter Blitz	£1.50	☐

Caroline Akrill
Eventer's Dream	£1.50	☐
A Hoof in the Door	£1.50	☐
Ticket to Ride	£1.50	☐

Michel Parry (ed)
Superheroes	£1.25	☐

Ulick O'Connor
Irish Tales and Sagas	£2.95	☐

To order direct from the publisher just tick the titles you want and fill in the order form.

All these books are available at your local bookshop or newsagent, or can be ordered direct from the publisher.

To order direct from the publishers just tick the titles you want and fill in the form below.

Name _____

Address _____

_____

Send to:
Dragon Cash Sales
PO Box 11, Falmouth, Cornwall TR10 9EN.

Please enclose remittance to the value of the cover price plus:

UK 45p for the first book, 20p for the second book plus 14p per copy for each additional book ordered to a maximum charge of £1.63.

BFPO and Eire 45p for the first book, 20p for the second book plus 14p per copy for the next 7 books, thereafter 8p per book.

Overseas 75p for the first book and 21p for each additional book.

Dragon Books reserve the right to show new retail prices on covers, which may differ from those previously advertised in the text or elsewhere.